IF YOU'VE GOT THE
MONEY
I'VE GOT THE
CRIME

IF YOU'VE GOT THE MONEY I'VE GOT THE CRIME

C.M. MCGUIRE

Beer For My Corpses

If You've Got the Money, I've Got the Crime

<u>The Kin</u> by Ethan A. Cooper

All Hail the Kin

Grillhome
Oldam's Temple
Norrik
Raiders Sea
Icebite
Spirit Oyster River
The
Disn
Vikkan
Summervatn
Bachran
Krysuvik
Marleen
Tyrran
Summer Trades
Gradvar
Knarrax
Mirrik
Puppi
Green
Bramland River
Sheaf
Low Wood
Rousea
Witchpen
Rousland
Vale Arlean
Dulur
Arlea
Stead
Sejent
Sedrios
Whenn
Southlen
S
The Paradisals
Banqui
Port Placid
Kindfish
Hull
N
W
E
S

Full-color map at KevinPettway.com

For my dad.
You're the reason I learned to love stories.
You also would have hated how gay this is going to get.

CHAPTER

ONE

Pickett mucked the stables.

Up until about a week ago, she hadn't been a stable mucker. Before that, she'd cleaned the kitchens, until the kitchen master of the Elowey Estate discovered that Pickett had been chipping at the sugar cones in the larder and selling the spoils at a discount. Not that he had the higher ground to stand on, considering he'd kept the coins he'd discovered tucked into the sole of Pickett's shoe as he growled at her.

"You should consider yourself lucky you even got here. Could've been sent to sea to hunt pirates, you could've been."

Before that, she'd actually been a housemaid. Until the lady's maid was sick and Lady Elowey asked Pickett to do her hair—a poor fucking decision on all counts that ended with Lady Elowey donning a suddenly shorter haircut and Pickett being removed from sight. She'd kept Elowey's copper hair comb though. Lady Elowey wouldn't be needing it anytime soon, and Pickett knew someone back home who would probably like it.

As she was dismissed from sight, Lady Elowey snapped at

her. "You should be more grateful. A brothel could've bought your debt instead of us."

That was an entirely fair observation, but clearly Lady Elowey cared more about her hair than decorum because she actually spit on Pickett's shoes. That just went to show how fancy the fancy folk truly were.

When it came right down to it, the stables were probably where Pickett belonged anyway. The stink of the stables was a little like the stink of the swamps. It was everywhere, even when she tried to focus on fresh hay. It was created largely by animals who didn't give a single copper shim that they'd caused it. More than any of that, it was the sort of place where someone like Pickett inevitably ended up. She could lie and say she was destined for glass windows and crystal goblets, but half-orphaned brats seldom saw them.

She did have a treasure, though. It was just waiting for her to finish her tenure in this estate and she'd be back to it.

Probably. Unless Fistic, Southfen's most powerful money-lender somehow decided three months of indentured servitude wasn't enough for him—which he just might. He was that very sort of rich bastard. The last couple of months, Pickett had spent far too much time trying to decide what to do if her time was up and Fistic dumped more shit on her.

But that was life, wasn't it? A kick in the teeth that left one toothless, unless you were rich enough to buy dentures.

She just hoped Edie had been all right these last couple of months. As far as Pickett knew, Edie had never been entirely on her own, much less responsible for running a ramshackle swamp bar without even the so-called Swamp Witch's reputation to protect her. Sure, Edie had gone and convinced a bunch of idiots that she was a master assassin, but how far would that really go? She wished the Eloweys had allowed her to receive mail.

Pickett stabbed the shovel hard into the packed earth of the stable floor, but she barely even managed to nick it. Rich assholes like this clearly wanted only the best, even for the floors their animals shit on. It was tempting to stab at it again and again, but that was a waste of energy. When her indentured contract began, she'd made a single promise to herself: to do as little as possible until the clock ran out.

When Fistic had sold her service to the Elowey family, that had been that. He got the money she owed him, they got three months of service, and Pickett got a sentence she simply had to serve. It was entirely feasible to fart around for three months doing the bare minimum. Unless something went wrong. The bar could have fallen into further disrepair. The lull in business could have been too much for Edie to handle without Pickett. Or worse. If the bar failed, she might be forced out. Pickett had always been able to protect herself by claiming she was a witch. A couple of months ago, Edie had claimed she was an assassin. Sure, she technically killed a man in self defense, but she just didn't have Pickett's flair for show-manship. If people saw through the lie, they might hassle her, rob from her, or turn her out of the bar and leave her stranded and homeless.

The thought of Edie made Pickett's heart clench and she slammed her shovel into the muck again. How much was Edie going through out there on her own?

Because Pickett's day was already going swimmingly, the door opened, and in waltzed one of the long-time Elowey servants. Pickett didn't know his name and, since he had a tendency to side eye her like some sort of bedraggled stray, she'd taken to calling him "Spidernose" for the very hairy mole just above one of his nostrils. The one time he'd caught her saying it, her usual dinner portion of fish and rice was replaced with old clams. Pickett had wisely chosen to go without that night.

Since being moved to the stables, she'd been hopeful not to

have to see Spidernose again. But the gods clearly liked to point and laugh at her specifically.

"What now?" she demanded, leaning on her shovel. "You can't possibly reprimand me for cleaning horse shit wrong."

"Don't underestimate my creativity," he said dryly before holding out a letter. "This is your writ of service stating the exact financial amount on your contract."

Oh fuck. They weren't going to charge her for the sugar or, gods forbid, the comb? Edie might be alone for a whole year at this rate.

"Much to the delight of myself and all staff of standing on this estate," he continued, "I am thrilled to announce that you no longer work here."

Pickett's cheeks burned. "You've got to be joking," she growled. "One month left on my contract. You can't sell it with one month left!"

Spidernose's lip curled into a chilly grin. "Oh? Is your contract not the property of Lady Elowey? They can do with it as they please. And you're lucky she didn't sell you off already. That pompous moneylender Fistic thought he was properly funny selling us such a worthless servant."

"I'll have you know I . . ." But Pickett had to bite her tongue. She didn't have the witch reputation out here. The ruse was as flimsy as dried seaweed away from the bar with her powders and effects.

"Ah. If only you'd learned to hold your tongue like that when you first arrived, it might have been more pleasant for all of us." He waved the letter aside. "Now kindly set aside the shovel."

Pickett raised the shovel in the air and dropped it on the ground, spraying bits of hay and filth across the half-cleaned stable and snatched the letter from his hand.

"So, who'd they sell me off to?" she demanded, unfolding the letter. "Brothel? Pirate hunters? I'm sure there's a rat catcher who'd love to set me loose on the streets of . . ."

She paused, reading over the fresh scrawl at the bottom of the writ. Then she read it over again, just to make sure she had it right.

The deposit of funds into the account of one S. Pickett has resulted in the contract's transfer to its new owner. The aforementioned individual is to make haste to her new place of employment, the Pick's Pocket. Failure to do so within a fortnight will result in an increase of the debt to be determined by the new owner of the debt.

She was going home. She was going home! Tits and teeth, what had Edie done? No. It didn't matter. That was a problem for when she got there.

"In that case, pleasure to never see you again." Pickett grinned, gave Spidernose a rude gesture, and all but skipped past him to the door.

At least until he could clear his throat. "Excuse me. Isn't there something you need to return?"

Fuck! Well, fine. Edie had the rest of her contract, now, so it didn't matter. If they charged her for this, then it would just transfer into debt they could work to pay off in some other creative way. He officially could not sell her to pirate hunters.

Pickett made to reach for her pocket when Spidernose continued, "That vest is property of the Elowey estate, and I am very certain you can't afford to replace it. Hand it over."

Pickett glanced down at the bold Elowey crest still emblazoned on her chest. Right. That. Funny how easy it was to forget after a few months of wearing it every day. She unfastened the front and tossed it to him.

"May your next hire have a stronger tolerance for horse shit."

Spidernose wrinkled his spidery nose as he caught the vest and began folding it.

"You should learn some gratitude," he said stiffly. "I'm not familiar with this establishment you're headed to, but it's better than the alternatives. If you don't shape up, they may just sell your contract to one of those new swamp establishments."

Pickett arched a brow. "Swamp establishments, you say?"

"Yes." He draped the vest over his arm and straightened. "I've heard people are trying to get business drumming out there. Can't imagine why. I've heard there are cannibals and demons. Even Rottering swamp supposedly has a witch."

Pickett opened her mouth and clapped one hand to her cheek. "Goodness me. You don't say."

Spidernose glowered. "You should take my advice. Clean up your act or that's right where you'll end up."

Pickett shrugged and stuffed her hands in her pockets as she turned to walk away.

"I don't know," she called over her shoulder. "Maybe a swamp is exactly where I belong."

CHAPTER

TWO

It had been a while since Pickett could freely walk through the streets of Southfen. Of course, without her old cape, she couldn't do it with the same swagger as she had in the past. But she was a free woman. If she could get the bar halfway profitable, she could get a new one, a more colorful one. And Edie could embroider all sorts of little pictures into the cape to help cement the "swamp witch" persona.

As she always did on her way out of town, she made a point of walking down the pleasure street. The cobbled road made it all the easier for drunken sailors to stumble from one establishment to another. The nicest establishment, of course, was the Spotted Dick.

Pickett paused outside of it, taking in the whitewash and the flowers in the windows. It had never looked nicer. Something inside of her ached. It wasn't that the Dick Dames were undeserving of a clean, fancy, bustling business. It was just so different. Sometimes, it felt like the world changed so fast a long blink could reshape it all.

Her attention was pulled away by a sudden pressure on her

pocket. Without even having to glance down, Pickett caught the little dip's wrist.

"Scram," she told him. "There's nothing in there, anyway."

The kid stuck his tongue out at her before yanking his hand free and scampering into an alley. Less of a dip and more of a rummage, he must have been new to thieving. But it was nice to see that some things in Southfen never changed.

She made her way to the edge of town, where the haphazard cobblestones and gravel faded into the dirt. The distant reek of the swamp was like slipping into a well-worn, newly darned pair of socks. Pickett breathed deep the perfume of mud and rot. Now all she needed was a cart to bum a ride on.

Picket glanced about. Nobody in the area, but there was something new. A wooden sign nailed to a tree. She walked up to it, and the writing made her lip curl.

ROAD WORK COMING
BYPASS THE SWAMP BOARDWALKS
ANTICIPATE TOLLS

Mother taint! When she'd gone into service, the road had been just a rumor. Clearly some rich someone was determined to ruin her business. Pickett yanked at the sign. When it didn't budge, she jumped up, planting her feet on the tree. The wood creaked and, little by little, she could feel the nails loosening.

Wheels rumbled over the dry grass and dirt. Pickett glanced up, just in time for the sign to fully pop free of the tree. She crashed to the ground in a terrific heap, just as the cart rolled to a stop next to her head. Pickett found herself staring up at a burly man and a cloaked woman, her brown-red skirt sticking out from the bottom of her cloak.

Pickett shoved the sign into the brush and scrambled to her feet, brushing dried leaves from her hair.

"Afternoon. I don't suppose you'd be willing to give a weary traveler a ride into the Rottering swamp?"

The cloaked woman leaned over, whispering something into the man's ear. He chuckled and turned to Pickett. "Say. Wanna tell us what you did to the sign?"

Pickett glanced back at the tree, now sporting two fresh holes in the bark. "I don't see any sign."

The cloaked woman's hand twitched under her cloak, and a loud *crack* cut through the air. Pickett only just managed to jump to the side as a mid-sized branch tumbled from the tree. Its leaves were still half green.

"The fuck?" Pickett breathed, as the driver laughed and the cart carried on. Absolute pricks. For a wild moment, she was inclined to think the woman with the bloody skirt had made it happen, but that was too unlikely. They'd had a magic-user just a few months ago, which was probably all the excitement this swamp would see in the next century. Another would be like the swamp had a lure for them.

Just another human asshole, which meant she could deal with it like she'd deal with any human asshole. Pickett scrambled to dig for a rock in the grass, but by the time she found a good-sized one, the cart was out of her range.

"Could've just said no," she muttered.

The odds the cloaked woman had caused the branch to fall were slim, but strange things existed in this world. Just a couple of months ago, a man had brought all the dead of the swamp back to life. Who was to say what a proper sorceress could do? If indeed the woman was that. Gods and other related dickheads knew Pickett could respect well-timed luck.

She wished whatever god was listening might be willing to fuck them over before she headed toward the boardwalks herself, bouncing the stone from hand to hand. The first step brought with it a soft creak as an old, rotted board cracked under her foot, splinters dropping into the fetid waters below.

Pickett blinked, then leaned on it again to be sure. Yes, that was definitely a rotted plank, and close to shore. Usually one of the villages maintained the boardwalks near them. It was a winning situation for everyone. In only two months, had they already given up on its maintenance?

"Well then." Pickett planted her hands on her hips and sighed. "I suppose I'll have to do my own work to keep this venture going."

She bounced the stone from hand to hand as she ambled toward the swamp. On the edge of the boardwalk, near where the water grasses began to thin out, sat a villager, his legs crossed and a crude fishing rod in his hand. He glanced her way, then gasped, dropping the rod into the water as he scrambled to his feet.

"Swamp witch," he gasped.

Pickett gripped the stone a little tighter.

"Yes?"

"I-I am sorry. I meant no offense." He ripped his straw hat from his head and crushed it between his fingers. "My village. Gristlark. There is no work there so I thought to try fishing for pips and shims and . . . Please, I request a blessing, swamp witch. Or-or whatever witches give out as blessings. Or a charm. Or a good fortune upon my miserable head."

Interesting. Still, it was good to know that her reputation went for something.

"Yeah sure." She tossed the rock to him. He didn't strike her as a guy who needed a whole show. "Keep it on your person and it may just bring you luck. Not in fishing, though. Without a rod, you're fucked."

They both glanced down at the base of the rod just bobbing above the fetid water, and drifting further with each second. The villager pressed the rock to his chest and bowed deeply.

"I-I thank you, swamp witch. Please. What can I do to repay you?"

Pickett planted her hands on her hips. "Got a cart?"

THREE

The deep orange of dusk was just starting to streak across the sky by the time the villager dropped her off, still singing her praise as he kissed the rock. At least she'd made someone happy.

She stood just outside the door, taking the building in for a long moment. The Pick's Pocket had always been a squat little shack in the middle of the swamp, intersected by a few creaking boardwalks. Part of its charm was that it was a dive with absolutely no competition because nobody else was crazy enough to open a bar there. Even after a bunch of sailors fixed the place up in return for booze, she knew every splintery board and cracked window like her own palm.

What loomed before her was not her bar.

The peeling wooden walls had been sanded down into something smooth and nice and painted over in olive-green, perfect to hide any mold or algae that would inevitably creep up the sides. The roof had been freshly thatched. Wooden cleats jutted out from the walkways, to which no less than five fishing boats were tied. Music and conversation drifted out through the small holes that served as windows. She half expected to see glass. Its absence was the only reassurance that her bar hadn't been completely unmoored and replaced with whatever the fuck this was.

Magda's perfect tits or ass or whatever the goddess was so good at having. If someone had hijacked her bar and made it better, she was going to be pissed.

Pickett shoved her way through the door. At least the inside was familiar. There were a few actual art pieces on the wall, but they weren't good. They looked like colorful blobs from young artists who'd only just started their apprenticeship, but in rural Sedrios it was nothing short of fine culture. A few tattered rugs had been draped over the spots where the wood floor had been patched. A young man with a scar stretching from his ear to his nose sat on the stage, plucking at the strings of a lute. He wasn't good, but he was fancy. And half the crowd watched him with quiet appreciation.

Half the *crowd*. Since when did her bar attract crowds?

Pickett picked through the tables. There were a few familiar merchants and fishermen, but many of these new patrons looked like they belonged in the seedy back alleys of Southfen. From the light of the candles—and somehow every table now had its own candle in a jar—the scars on most of their faces were evident. Half the room dressed in dark clothes with knives and swords slung around their waists. Maybe it was the fact that everyone was armed, but a couple of them sat in the back corner playing at dice without any rancor. Best of all, nobody had decided to bring in their goat or a bucket of fish. All these terri-fying-looking customers behaved perfectly. On top of every-thing, the place didn't stink. It smelled of baked bread which undercut the familiar reek of human sweat and spilled alcohol. It was everything she'd ever wanted the Pick's Pocket to be.

What the actual ever-shitting fuck?

The song ended and the scarred young man stood, dipping into a curt bow as the crowd applauded and cheered for him.

"Yeah, Grimstalk!"

"Knew you could do it, mate!"

"Proud of you, man!"

It was like waking up from a fever dream only to discover the dream was the most tame and mundane thing going on. She watched the young, mediocre lute player "Grimstalk" slink back to a table where everybody actually clapped him on the shoulder. She stared for a long moment, waiting for someone to pull a knife in case they were buttering him up. Knives she could handle. A yell, a threat, a sleight of hand to convince them she was a swamp witch to scare some wits into them and regain control. But there was no knife. Just a conversation while cards were spread out on the table for another hand.

"Pickett!" a young voice shouted.

Pickett turned to see a half-fed scoundrel of a boy scamper from behind the bar and up to her, his eyes wide.

"Letterboy?" she said, catching his chin. "You here delivering letters, boy?"

"Not anymore. Edie gave me a job!" He beamed. "She gave me a bed in the kitchen and all."

Did she now? Pickett turned the boy's chin left and right. Still a skinny little scrap of a thing, but he was clean. His ragged clothes were patched. Fuck, Edie had taken in the stray, hadn't she?

"And where is Edie?"

"Lemme get her!" Letterboy gave a little jump then ducked away, darting through the crowds until she couldn't spy him anymore.

Another performer took to the stage. This one was a tall woman with what appeared to be a wooden leg. She dragged a chair up behind her so she could sink down as she began to sing.

"Me feller were pretty, but sharp were his teeth.
Him face it were gentle but harsh underneath.
He'd tell me that I had tae fondle him carrot,
But when it was my turn he just wouldna hear it!"

The bar erupted in laughs and cheers, but one voice pierced through them all.

"Pickett!"

Pickett's heart swelled up so big she could hardly breathe. She turned just in time to see a pale woman with straw-blond hair racing toward her. Edie! Edie was here. Whatever happened, it was okay. If Edie was behind it, Pickett didn't care if she'd gone and turned the bar into a tea room. If it came from Edie, it was exactly what Pickett wanted.

She had only a moment to brace herself as Edie launched herself forward. And fuck! She smelled good, like hops and fresh baked bread. And there was a little more force behind that hug. Pickett had to catch her breath as Edie took a step back to beam at her. She had a little more weight on her, like she'd been eating properly the last few months. It filled her out into something healthy. And there was color in her cheeks. And Pickett couldn't spot any holes in her clothes. Was that a new dress? Well why not? If Edie could afford to paint the bar and buy more candles, why couldn't she afford to buy herself something nice?

Like the contract. Fuck.

"Edie, are you why I got out a month early?"

Edie grinned and winked at her. Pickett blinked. In just two months, Edie had turned Pick's Pocket into a decent establishment and earned enough money to clean up the bar and buy off a third of Pickett's debt. How quickly things changed.

Pickett had to catch her breath for a moment before she shook her head. "The hell did you do to my bar?"

Edie's grin turned wicked as she winked. "I know you love it."

"But there are acts on." She gestured behind her. "Why aren't you going around collecting tips?"

"Is that all you want to talk about?" Edie grabbed Pickett's hands and tugged her close. "Can't we celebrate that you're home?"

"I mean sure, but"—Pickett glanced at the full crowd—"home is different and-and can you be away from the bar?"

"Letterboy has it under control." Edie gestured behind her to the waif of a boy sitting behind the bar, sliding a beer to a man wearing a skull mask.

Pickett wrinkled her nose. "Weren't you the one opposed to the squirt having a drink?"

"Oh, he knows better than to try." Edie leaned forward, her blue eyes wide and glittering with mischief. "The last time he tried, two bounty hunters confiscated it and hog-tied him for me."

As funny as the image was, Pickett had to frown. "Bounty hunters? Did you waste money hiring bounty hunters on Letterboy?"

Edie cocked her head to one side and fixed Pickett with an even stare. "Come on. You know I wouldn't do that. Look around. Everyone here wants to keep this place in good working order. It's practically the new guild headquarters."

It took Pickett a moment to sort out what, exactly, that meant. When it finally settled in her brain, she reeled back and turned to stare at the peg-legged woman on the stage who looked like she could kill almost anyone in the room with that very leg.

"Are-are we a bounty hunter bar now?"

Edie beamed and grabbed Pickett's hand. "Come on. Let me show you the other draw."

She dragged Edie to the back corner, where the sole dice set used to be. In its place was a series of shelves, each of which had a few cages on them, a plaque next to each with only a few words, doubtless so their only sort-of literate guests could better interpret the meaning.

"Whisper Grass," Pickett read as she frowned at a lump of long-dried swamp grass. "Wait. Is this some of the swamp grass the Northfellow used for that spell that brought the dead back?"

Edie nodded. "Unfortunately, not a lot of people believe it's real."

"It's the most magical thing in this place," Pickett muttered under her breath, wrinkling her nose at the distant memory of the sound of the whisper and the sight of the half-decomposed bodies drifting through the water. It was a good thing the grass was dry and dead, even if she missed the Northfellow sloshing away his rum at the bar.

"People think only trolls can do whisper magic." Edie shrugged and pointed at another little cage. "Funny enough, that one's really popular. I had to move the table away from this corner because people kept wanting to touch it."

Pickett wrinkled her nose and leaned forward to peer at what was plainly a turtle skull with a few plaster horns clumsily sculpted onto it. The plaque read "Dragon skull."

"Can dragons even survive in swamp water?" Pickett asked.

"Probably not. But business has never been better." Edie tapped the nose of the skull and grinned. "This here is a little good luck charm."

Yeah, that sounded fake. Pickett frowned at the suddenly less-than-rowdy bar. So maybe this particular bounty hunting guild was well-behaved, enough to keep even the fishermen and merchants in line, but surely even they didn't have the coin to transform this place so drastically.

The peg-legged woman dipped in a disgruntled curtsy to mild applause before limping off the stage, only to be replaced by a burly man holding a cat.

"How is business this good, exactly?"

"Oh you know," Edie said airily. "They think I'm a master

assassin and that you're a powerful swamp witch who stopped the undead invasion a few months ago. They want to come and see the place where we work." She nudged Pickett. "Now that you're back, it'll be twice as busy."

"Edie."

"I mean, it hasn't all been steady. Last month someone with a cloak paid with a satchel of teeth. That wasn't great. But we could afford the loss."

"Edie!"

Pickett caught her hand, and Edie met her eyes. "Let's wait until they leave." Edie nodded toward the guests.

Pickett's heart jumped in her throat. "Edie, you bought my contract with a month left on it. That takes money."

Edie twisted her wrist to give Pickett's hand a squeeze. "Later," she mouthed before tugging her away from the makeshift museum and toward the kitchen. A kitchen now packed with actual cooking equipment. Edie flitted about like a dragonfly on the reeds as she pointed out this and that.

"I traded this cutting board for a mug of beer. I think it was just weighing the trader down, honestly. Oh, and this new pan? The owner just really wanted a witch's favor. I tried telling him you weren't here, but he said an acquaintance was good enough. And this." She brandished a long, gleaming knife, albeit in a bizarre shape. "Supposedly it's kohmium, and it's indestructible. Look." She banged the knife a few times on the side of the potbelly stove and held it up. "Not even a little bit dull. If the tinker is right, I'll never need another knife as long as I live."

"It looks like your people skills are paying off," Pickett breathed, glancing around until her eyes landed on a half-depleted bowl of rolls. Just the sight of them made her mouth water.

"You can afford yeast?" she asked. Obviously Edie could afford flour. She could afford rugs and candles and cleats and a paint job on the exterior. Why wouldn't she be able to afford yeast?

"Everyone wants to call them travelers rolls, but I wanted to brand these for us," Edie said, snatching one and shoving it into Pickett's hand. "I call them pocket rolls."

Pickett sniffed the warm bread before taking a bite. It was a proper roll on the outside, but inside was a medley of minced mudfish and gravy and spice. She let out the little moan of pleasure before she could think to bite it back. Fuck that was good.

She chewed, swallowed, bit, chewed and swallowed again, then demolished the roll before she blinked at Edie.

"Are we respectable?"

Edie grinned back at her.

USUALLY THE CROWDS dissipated on their own. The Pick's Pocket didn't rent out rooms so they either had to row their fishing boats back to their homes or else find a room to rent in a nearby village. That was normal. What wasn't was the fact that they all left on their own, many of them well before the bar actually closed. And they left their tables in good order too.

"The head of their guild has strict guidelines for public behavior," Edie explained as she wiped down the bar. It didn't look much cleaner, but it was kind of nice to consider that this was now the sort of place worth keeping clean.

"And they actually behave?"

"If they want to be part of the best guild on the continent, they do."

Edie ducked down then rose, dragging a groggy Letterboy up by his skinny wrist. "Come on, you."

Pickett followed a few steps behind, watching silently as Edie led Letterboy to a little cot in the back of the kitchen. It didn't just have a blanket and pillow, though. As Letterboy settled into it, he had to push some things out of the way: a slate and chalk, a clumsily carved wooden slingshot, and a rag that had been tied off in a few places to form a sort of doll. Edie handed Letterboy the doll rag before plucking the lantern off the wall and nodding to the back.

"Have we adopted him?" she whispered.

Edie shrugged. "One foundling to another. I know it's no fun having nowhere to belong. So I thought he could belong here too."

"Soft."

"If I'm soft, it just makes me a nice place to land." Edie grinned at her before pushing open the door to their room.

It was nice to see some things didn't change. It was still an oversized closet with a couple of cots set up. The blankets had been patched. Edie's side had a few more books. Besides that, it felt like home.

Pickett heaved a happy sigh and plopped down onto her cot, toeing off her boots. "I was half afraid you'd go and paint this room too."

"Some things have to stay the same for you to see how far you've come." Edie began unlacing her bodice. "Besides. I used to sleep with the cows when I was a milkmaid. It's not exactly un-cozy to share a room with someone."

"Especially when that someone is a peach like me." Pickett rolled onto her side and winked.

Edie sniggered and shrugged off her bodice, then shimmied out of her skirt, leaving her in only a linen shift. A proper linen shift. The kind she'd never have been able to afford when Pickett had to funnel all their earnings into repairs and payments on the bar. It suited her. Nice things suited her.

For just a moment, the fine comb she'd nicked from the Elowey estate burned in her pocket. She itched to pull it out, to offer Edie something nice. But before she could reach for it, Edie reached under her cot and pulled out a bundle of fabric.

Pickett's heart skipped a beat. She took the bundle and shook it out. A few months ago, her trademark swamp witch look had been her patchwork cape. It had been lost during the undead crisis that had ended with Pickett's servitude. But this? This was like her old cape, but better. There was a thick set of front straps to drape over her chest and fasten behind her back. The fabric patched together looked like it had been cut from tailor scraps in every possible color, not scraps of used clothing. As she shook it out, the odd stitch along the trim caught the lantern light.

"The fuck are these?" Pickett ran her thumb over one of the stitched symbols. "These don't look like the runes on my old cloak."

"That's because these are real." Edie tugged a pamphlet from between a couple of her books and spread it wide. It showed a dozen different symbols, each of which showed a short descriptor.

Pickett glanced down at the runes, then back up. "You mean real magic? Not a con?"

"I think so." Edie shrugged and smiled shyly down at the pamphlet. "It's not extensive. But I heard people who can do this are called runecasters. And anyone can do it if they learn. So I thought it wouldn't hurt. I picked the runes for protection and stitched those in."

She'd stitched those in. Pickett sucked in a sharp breath. "Did you make this whole cloak yourself?"

"You think I'd waste money to hire someone else?"

Suddenly, the stolen comb felt like a tawdry offer in return. Edie had stitched a cloak for her with, well runes were questionable, but the intention was wonderful. And in return, all she could offer was a stolen treasure she'd nicked due to fucking up at her job.

Pickett hugged the cloak a little closer and smiled, searching for a desperate place to pivot. It only took a couple of seconds to find a better place to focus.

"Who is your investor?"

"Ours," Edie said evenly, but she shrugged, and one corner of her shift slid over her pale shoulder. There were a couple more freckles since Pickett had last seen her.

"Fine. Who's this investor of ours?"

"His name is Bresk." Edie played with the front of her pamphlet. "He came on one of the busier nights. Apparently, he'd heard about the famous swamp witch and wanted to meet you. I mean, he was disappointed not to, but he said he saw the potential in this place. Sent money and supplies to fix it up and attract business."

Something about the name Bresk tickled the back of Pickett's brain in a way she couldn't quite scratch.

Pickett frowned. "There's a new road coming in. Half the merchants and fishermen who used to come here were scared off by the undead and—"

"And the fact that you're a fake witch and I told them I'm an assassin." Edie leaned her cheek on one hand. "Who cares? We have a whole guild using this place for their meet-ups and they're amazing customers. They'll probably keep coming despite the road."

"This Bresk person thinks that?" Pickett scoffed. "I think he's trying to sell you a fart and calling it incense."

"He's not selling, he's investing," Edie insisted. "He's not asking for a return for a whole year, and the rate is good. Thanks to him I could clean up the bar, buy better stock, buy your contract, and on top of all of that we're both going to bed tonight with full bellies. So far, it's working out better than the loan you took from Fistic."

That was true. Even so, the whole situation still made Pickett's gut clench.

"It's too good to be true."

"Yeah. I'm not used to good things happening to me either." Edie's smile softened. Under the lamplight, with her straw-yellow hair hanging down around her face, wearing only a shift that fit her properly, she looked so lovely. It was tempting to lean forward and kiss her. What would Edie taste like? Pocket rolls and rum, or something else wonderful? What would Edie feel like pressed up against her?

"Just give it some time," Edie said. "After a year, he'll be back. You can meet him. It'll be perfect."

Pickett swallowed and shoved the urge down as she draped the new cape around her shoulders. Stupid notion. So much had changed already. They could both use a little normalcy.

"I suppose you've done well with this place." Pickett winked as she fastened the clasp around her throat then rose. "I'll go keep watch for the night."

Edie's expression fell. "What? No. You just got home. You had a long trip today."

"Yeah, but I want to get back into the rhythm of things." She hesitated then gave Edie's shoulder a squeeze. "Consider it thanks for what you did to this place."

"Fine. But in the morning, you sleep in. Once we make a little more money, I'm going to get proper locks put in so we don't even have to keep watch anymore."

"Fine. If I must." Pickett turned with a flourish of her new cape. Time to stretch some old muscles. Sedrios had been without its swamp witch two months too long.

FOUR

The rhythm of Pick's Pocket had changed. With less care needed to dream up ways to make quick repair cash or patch up holes in the floor or wall, they could actually dedicate time to upkeep. Every day, all the tables and floors were wiped down. Edie began kneading dough to bake the pocket rolls and whatever else she cared to serve in the evening, and they all sat down to three proper meals a day.

They could afford three proper meals a day. No wonder Edie had filled out. At this rate all three of them would be plump as pampered pigs. Even the tobacco for Pickett's pipe was good stuff. When she'd taken her first puff of it, she hadn't even realized for that first moment the smoke filled her lungs. It was too smooth, too sweet, too fine for someone like her. But Edie just beamed and asked if she liked it.

Yeah, she did. If she wasn't careful, she was going to get very, very used to this kind of living.

Every day brought a new chore and a new way of doing things.

Pickett went to add water to the rum but no. It turned out they made more money when they didn't do that.

When they placed the order for their beer barrels, they no longer chose the cheapest options.

She didn't even need to pull out any of her tricks. No sparks, no blackout bottles, no false witchcraft whatsoever. It wasn't necessary. Their new clientele actually managed to get through their cups without spilling half of it on the ground or breaking each others' noses.

After a couple of weeks back home, Pickett found herself in what used to be an unusable closet due to the rickety floor. Now it was a toilet. Edie called it a "water closet" because that's what she'd read about in some book about fancy people. But it was a toilet, a proper toilet, where guests could go rather than just pissing off the docks right into the water.

"Every morning, Edie has me take the bucket far down the boardwalks to dump it so it doesn't stink up the water around the bar," Letterboy explained as he scrubbed said bucket.

Pickett wiped down the walls, where someone had carved "Fuck skinflint whore bosses" and someone else carved "Fucking your ma is wrong," along with a few other messages in languages she couldn't read. Pickett briefly considered chipping away at them before making the executive decision to leave them. It gave the place a little more character.

She glanced down at Letterboy. He'd gained a little weight too. He still looked like an urchin but no longer a skeletal one.

"Do you like it here?"

Boy glanced up at her, then nodded. "Edie's nice."

"And you don't miss earning pennies as a messenger in Southfen?"

He grinned and shook his head. "I just spent what I got on food, anyway. Here, there's food every day and I can earn pips from folk who come in. I've got my own bed and everything."

Something lit up in his face. Something that made her tremble inside. She knew what he must be feeling and how amazing it all felt. Lucky for Letterboy, Edie could probably give him everything he thought he was getting. Pickett opened a bar, but Edie turned it into a home.

"So you're saying you're happy?"

"Ain't been in a scrape in months. Happiest I've ever been."

Pickett ruffled his hair and gave his shoulder a little shove. "Go help Edie in the kitchen and stay out of any scrapes while you're in there."

Letterboy scurried off and Pickett trudged into the main bar area to take stock of their rum and bibblewood juice. Business had been good, but they weren't going to get another rum shipment for a while. As good as their bounty hunting clientele were, she expected they'd be far less pleasant without the alcohol.

A grimy little face peered through the cracked window, crumpled paper clutched in his hand. At the sight of her, the kid perked up and started banging on the wooden frame. Great. News from Southfen. Not so long ago, it would have been Letterboy doing this job. It was only inevitable that a new urchin would take his place.

"Edie!" Pickett called as she headed to the door. "Fetch a coin, we have mail!"

There was a clatter from the kitchen, and Edie and Letterboy hurried out. Pickett opened the door and the new urchin slid in, the paper still clutched in his grubby hand. Letterboy's face darkened. Before either Pickett or Edie could grab him, he launched himself at the urchin. Both boys hit the floor in a flurry of kicks and punches, growling and snapping like dogs. The letter went flying.

So much for staying out of scrapes. Pickett might have cheered him on, except she and Edie were taking care of the boy. If he broke his wrist, it would become their problem. She jumped into the fray, hauling Letterboy off, even as he bucked and kicked and shouted obscenities. Edie knelt down next to the urchin, who glowered and spat a bloody wad onto the floor.

"The fucker stole my spot!" Letterboy shouted.

"Hey. Calm down." Pickett shoved him into a chair and leaned over him, keeping him loosely contained.

Letterboy hunched over, seething as he glared past her ribs, and in that moment she could see the grimy thing he used to be. The desperate, hungry messenger who popped into the bar every so often with a message and an open palm. There was a wildness there that didn't go away after a few good meals.

"You live here now," she said firmly.

"But he stole my spot," Letterboy growled. "My pallet. My whole stash of food. My blanket."

"Yeah?" Pickett cupped his chin, forcing his gaze upward. "Look where you are now."

He set his jaw. "But I—"

"Look where you are now," she repeated. "You've got a bed here. You get three meals a day. You just said you're the happiest you've ever been. Do you think he's got it as good?"

The fire burning behind Letterboy's eyes dimmed. After a moment, he averted his gaze.

"Go clean the kitchen. Dump the anger out with the dishwater."

Letterboy opened his mouth, then closed it and gave a sullen nod. Pickett straightened. He rose and trudged sullenly to the kitchen but, to his credit, didn't spare the urchin another look.

Edie still knelt next to the boy, the letter clutched in her hand, but her expression hardened a little.

"It sounds like you stole our boy's sleeping spot," she said.

The urchin wiped his bloodied lip and glowered. "It's his own fault for not guarding it."

"You little—"

"Give him his coin, Edie."

Edie scowled, but pulled a shim from her apron pocket and dropped it in his hand. The boy took it and rose, stomping out the door.

"I'd have thought you of all people would want to turn him out empty-handed," Edie scoffed, in the way of someone who'd always had a roof over her head.

"He got the licks he deserved. Maybe now Letterboy's got it out of his system. And speaking of letters."

Edie carried the crumpled scrap of paper to the bar and smoothed it out against the rough surface.

"Requesting the service of the swamp witch," she read aloud. "Potential job offer resulting in glorious funds. Eagerly awaiting a positive response in Room Four of the Fair Fishman."

Now that was strange.

"Why hire me?" Pickett muttered.

Edie arched a brow. "You're the swamp witch."

"I made that story up to keep people out of my business, not advertise my services." She shook her head. "There's got to be more to this. I mean, is this your investor?"

"No. He could come by anytime. Certainly he could announce himself, no messenger necessary." Edie turned to face her, a coy smile tugging at her lips. "Pickett, the last time a strange opportunity presented itself, I got an investor who helped me turn this place around."

"You think we should just jump at every opportunity?" Pickett scoffed. "It's too risky."

"I mean"—Edie wrinkled her nose as she glanced at the letter and back at Pickett—"wasn't it a risk for me to get an investor?"

"Edie—"

"What about the awful loan you got for this place from the start? Or you taking me in? Life is risk, Pickett." She stepped forward and squeezed Pickett's hands. "It's not a bad thing to trust."

Pickett squeezed her hands back. "Remember how my trust landed me in months of servitude?"

"If you don't trust him"—Edie took a step forward and

beamed like a summer sun—"then trust me. It's worth taking a chance. I can feel it."

It was like being punched right in her weak spot. Pickett considered fighting back, but what good would it do? That weak spot was right where Edie lived. She'd stuck around even after Pickett's secrets and debts had seen her indentured. She'd stuck around despite the chaos and drama of this place, and she'd made it better and given Letterboy a real place to belong.

"Damn it," Pickett muttered before hunting a quill to scratch out a response. "Letterboy! Do you want to go show off how well you're doing to all the other urchins in Southfen?"

Letterboy poked his head out of the kitchen and grinned so widely that blood started to trickle out of his bruised nose.

THAT NIGHT, their most popular performer to date arrived. He wasn't just loved because he knew how to sing and twirl around in a lacey skirt, though. Kellum was the bringer of rum—the life's blood of the Pick's Pocket.

"Oh thank good fuck," Pickett said, pushing past him to grab the first box of bottles and haul it inside. "Edie's got this place so busy, we're actually running low on beer. Never did that before. Unless it started to go green."

Kellum blinked at her. "Aren't you supposed to be toiling in some posh estate?"

"They let me go for good behavior."

"Right . . ." Kellum frowned, then glanced at the stage. "Are you good to finish loading and unloading things? I need to put my face on so I can perform."

"Gee, what a gallant gentleman you are," Pickett grunted as she hefted up another case.

Kellum grinned and gave his skirt an effeminate shake. "Not tonight, I'm not."

The little shit was becoming quite the diva. Pickett rolled her eyes, but she couldn't help smirking a bit as she went about unloading the rest of the rum shipment. From the bar main, the sound of strings filled the air. Soon enough, Kellum began to add his own unique spin on an old song, replacing the word "soul" with "hole" where most necessary. She secured the booze closet and the cart now filled with empty bottles before heading out. Already back from his delivery, Letterboy stood behind the bar, his chin just peeking over the edge, as he took orders for bounty hunters cheering on Kellum, who spun left and right across the stage, lute in hand. That summed up everyone Pickett knew. So who was her kitchen maid deep in conversation with? In the corner next to her miniature museum, Edie nodded at a man with thick, unruly hair tied back in a yellow ribbon. Something about him made Pickett's skin crawl.

"Edie?"

Edie turned with a bright smile. "Pickett! This is our potential business partner Simon."

Simon?

The curly-haired man turned around, his dark eyes sparkling as he grinned broadly. The gap between his front teeth was just a hair thicker than Pickett's.

"Sonora! I've missed you so much."

Pickett smashed her fist into his nose.

CHAPTER

FIVE

Y ou absolute cock!" Pickett snapped as Simon reeled back, his hands clasped over his nose as blood dribbled onto his lip.

"Tits, Nora, I thought you'd be happy to see me," he moaned, his voice muffled behind his hands.

"And whose fault is it that we haven't seen each other? Who dumped me like a sack of old radishes and took off?"

"I knew you were safe."

The crowd of the bar began to murmur, more eyes turning away from the stage and toward them. Kellum went pale, then cleared his throat and turned to the audience.

"Songs are all well and good," he squeaked, "but let me tell you about the one-eyed sailor. I saw him headed for a brothel. Pops out his wooden eye and opens it right up to reveal a jewel the size of my tooth. My *eye* tooth, if you catch my drift."

The audience rumbled with laughter and a few gazes turned back to the night's performer. Before Pickett could take another swing, Edie jumped between them.

"All right, whatever's going on, I'm sure it can be discussed better without violence," she said firmly. "Pickett—"

"What?" Both Pickett and the blood-faced backstabber said at once.

Edie's expression tightened. She shot Pickett a cold look, the likes of which could freeze her bowels. She did not, however, take a step back.

"My Pickett," she clarified. "Though I suppose that's not really your name."

"It is!" Pickett threw her hands in the air. "Just not my given one."

Edie's eyes narrowed. "Right. But you're not the only one with it. Were you planning on telling me you had a brother?"

"Not when I was very convinced I'd never see him again." Pickett glowered at Simon.

Edie huffed and planted her hands on her hips. "*Sonora.* If you could hold off from punching our potential business collaborator, I would just love that."

Pickett jabbed a finger at him. "Absolutely not. If he sent the messenger, then he can cook his letter and shove it down his—"

"That's enough." Edie gripped Pickett's shoulder. "Perhaps we should take this in the back. Away from listening ears."

Pickett scowled and glanced past Simon, where half the bounty hunters were covertly watching them by very pointedly looking anywhere else and the other half stared openly.

"Fine," she grumbled.

Simon glanced between them, his eyes watering before he straightened, his hands dropping to his side. Pickett was a little mollified to see his nose had gone crooked, if also disappointed that it looked like the bleeding was slowing already.

"Right." He cleared his throat, then winced. "Lead the way."

Edie led them back to the kitchen and, as soon as the door closed behind them, the distant buzz of conversation actually grew louder.

"Just what we need," Pickett grumbled. "Bottom feeding

bounty hunters butting in on our business. How many of them do you think will want in on whatever nonsense this is?"

"They aren't bottom feeders," Edie said.

At the same time Simon insisted, "It's not nonsense."

Edie pushed past him and planted her hands on her hips. "You're not in a position to be snippy right now, Pickett. We agreed no more secrets. Turns out you have secret family. What next, a secret pony?"

"He is no brother of mine." Pickett jabbed a finger in Simon's direction. "He stopped being that when he abandoned me in a brothel when I was twelve years old. Know who taught me how to sew? What my monthlies were? Checked that I knew my letters and numbers? Prostitutes. Not my family."

"They agreed to take you," Simon insisted, taking a big enough step back to remove him from range of Pickett's fist. "Papa was gone. We both know the creditors probably killed him. I was barely sixteen."

"Hang on." Edie held up a hand, first shooting Pickett a glare, then shooting one at Simon. "You left her in a brothel when she was twelve?"

Simon shrugged. "They promised they wouldn't put her to work. Not like that anyway."

"Mm." Edie crossed her arms. "Did you go back to visit her? Even once?"

Simon shifted from foot to foot, glancing away from Edie. "I kept tabs on her. And goodness, this kitchen is awfully small. With the money from this job, you could really fix this place up." He picked up the kohmium knife and used it to point at odds and ends. "Replace these walls. Bigger stove. Your larder ought to be three times this size if you really want this place to be a success."

"Big businessman coming in and telling us what to do. Give me that!" Pickett slapped his wrist and snatched the kohmium knife. "You can't just come back after all these years and pretend nothing happened."

Simon sighed, his shoulders sagging a little. "I know," he admitted. "But there is a job. There is real money in it."

"Just like there was always money in Papa's ventures, hm?"

Edie rested a hand on Pickett's arm. "I think now might not be the time for decisions. Come back in the morning, Simon."

Simon glanced between them. When Pickett didn't speak, he bobbed into a small bow. "Of course. I can bring some buns for breakfast."

He brushed past them, then paused at the door.

"For what it's worth, Sonora," he said. "It is good to see you again."

"Choke on a chestnut, Simon."

When the door closed, Edie began to rub Pickett's arm like someone might stroke a startled cat.

"I had no idea. I never would have let him in if I knew."

"And I didn't tell you." Pickett shook her head. "Just promise me he's not your secret investor."

"No, that's someone else," Edie said.

Good. The last thing she needed was to have Simon tied up in the bar. Pickett nudged the door open, narrowing her eyes as she saw Simon lingering by the entrance.

"It would be so easy," she muttered.

"Pickett, no."

"Just a few heavy rocks on the ankle. Maybe summon a swamp beast."

"Murder is a bad business decision, and you know it." She squeezed Pickett's shoulder. "And so is keeping things like this from me."

Pickett groaned inwardly. This was going to be a Thing now, wasn't it?

"I would have told you if I ever thought I'd see him again, Edie. I didn't even care if he was alive. Still don't."

Edie smiled and touched her cheek. "I adore you, but you are absolutely fucking stone-brained. Don't burn a bridge before it's built."

Pickett jerked her head away. "Oh? And would you want to build a bridge with whatever shit dumped you in Gallraven when you were a baby?"

"Absolutely."

Edie didn't even hesitate. Of course she didn't. She had that look in her eye, that set of her jaw. She was so certain of herself and the world. And maybe, just maybe, there was something to it. She'd trusted her mystery investor and the Pick's Pocket had never been in better shape.

More than that, it was the way she stared at Pickett with those wide eyes, the way she pursed her lips when she wanted something. Fuck, Edie made it hard to tell her no.

"Fine," Pickett turned back to the doorway. "I'll give Simon a shot. But if he pulls any stunts, I get to make sure he won't bother us again."

"I expect nothing less, Sonora."

Edie breezed past her, heading straight for Letterboy at the bar, who was pointing to his nose and loudly extolling the tale of his revenge to a pair of appreciative bounty hunters. Pickett watched her go, then surveyed the rest of the room until she spotted a familiar, punchable face. If they were going to work with Simon, it might not hurt to have a little extra muscle.

CHAPTER
SIX

I'm never one to say no to money, but isn't this a family matter?" Jodiah asked, cutting into an apple with a blade that had probably seen the insides of some poor bastard's gut. A true hero's breakfast. But what else could she expect from one of the rougher members of the bounty hunters' guild? At least this time he was here as a patron and not sniffing out trouble for Edie and Pickett. Probably. Last she'd checked, none of the shit villages near the swamp had any further cause to send him their way.

"Money's money," Pickett explained. "Once Simon's gone, he'll be as much family to me as you, and maybe we all come out richer."

Jodiah narrowed his eyes. "You're not planning on asking me to kill him, are you?"

"I just want you to make sure he doesn't run off on us again."

Jodiah grunted, which Pickett took as agreement. She nodded and poured a couple of slugs of rum into cracked glasses and toasted the new partnership, just as Edie and Letterboy shuffled out of the kitchen and into the bar proper, carrying a kettle and several wooden mugs between them.

"Isn't it a little early?" Edie scoffed, arching a brow at the glasses.

Jodiah chuckled and knocked back his drink by way of answer. Pickett sipped at hers as she played with the flints she always wore on her fingers. The spark they produced wouldn't be enough to scare off anyone who knew she wasn't really a witch, but it was nice to know she could light someone on fire if she wanted. Beyond that, Edie could play with runes now.

"Don't suppose any of your fancy new runes can be used to sprout an extra nose over Simon's ass?" Pickett asked as Edie and Letterboy set one of the tables.

Edie hummed and fixed Pickett with that stern look. "Afraid the pamphlet isn't that extensive. Sorry. Hiring a bodyguard will have to be enough."

"Good to feel appreciated," Jodiah said as he sauntered to the table, where he continued to slice up his apple.

Pickett joined them, and no sooner had her bottom graced the seat than the bar door opened and in walked the bastard himself. Simon had a dark ring under one of his eyes, branching off from an ugly spot on his nose. It gave her enough satisfaction to straighten up as she poured tea into the mugs.

Jodiah nibbled at his apple as he glanced between Simon and Pickett. Simon took his seat. Edie toyed with the laces on her bodice.

"Good morning," Simon said pleasantly.

"Good morning," Edie and Letterboy replied in unison.

Jodiah said nothing. Pickett glared.

Simon cleared his throat. "I, uh, see we have new friends joining this little venture. And one of them looks to be quite the scrapper."

He went to nudge Letterboy's shoulder, but Pickett caught his wrist and scowled.

"Don't talk to the boy," she said.

"Right." Simon straightened and forced a smile onto his face, which managed to make his bruising look a little worse. "And I take it Sonora decided to bring you on for a little extra muscle?"

Jodiah chewed slowly, maintaining eye contact with Simon. Fuck, he was good. Pickett might just have to offer him a tip.

Letterboy swung his legs back and forth and leaned forward onto the table as he spoke up. "So how much money are you paying us?"

"Letterboy," Edie scolded, but Simon grinned.

"That depends entirely on whether or not Sonora's willing to work with her own flesh and blood."

"Slightly less blood than yesterday," Pickett said tapping the side of her nose.

Simon cleared his throat and took his glass. "It was earned and hopefully gives us a chance for a fresh start." He raised his mug. "To our new business venture."

Nobody mirrored his action. Simon glanced from Pickett to Jodiah to Edie before, at last, Letterboy stood on his chair and leaned forward, clacking his own mug against it.

Edie smiled tightly. "Simon, I'm glad to say we've decided to move forward with your proposition. And may I thank you for giving us the opportunity to further improve this establishment."

"Yes, well." He turned to Pickett. "Had to jump at the chance to reconnect with my sister. Not to mention a magic user'll be a real boon on a job like this. Tell me, sister, how did you end up becoming a swamp witch in the first place?"

"By being as much a swindler as our father," Pickett grumbled.

Simon frowned. "Father was a great merchant, and I've followed in his footsteps."

"Mm. The busted nose proves that much."

"Anyway"—Edie set a hand on Pickett's forearm, her tone

going brittle—"we know why we're all here. Simon, tell us about the job."

Jodiah set the remains of his apple aside and leaned forward onto the table, lacing his fingers together. Simon wiggled a little in his seat and sat up, puffing his chest out like a bird. Pickett sank deeper in her seat, glaring daggers and longswords and plenty of arrows at him.

"The job is to liberate someone from her current conditions," Simon explained. "An interested party brought it to my attention that there is a maid only freshly twenty locked in the temple of Al-Dagos. He would very much like for us to remedy the situation."

Jodiah hissed and pressed a hand over his heart.

Pickett frowned. "Wait. Is that the god with the seven penises?"

"No no no," Edie whispered. "You're thinking Bukker. The dog. Al-Dagos is a dragon."

"Technically not even here," Pickett pointed out. "All the gods fucked off to the wherever-place, didn't they?"

"You shouldn't talk about them like that," Jodiah grumbled as he shifted in his seat. "And we shouldn't pinch from one of them. Why would the great dragon even have worshippers? The Untamed don't listen to us, and to seek their attention is to court blasphemy."

Simon's expression pinched. "Regardless, there is a temple to this particular god. And Nancy is stuck in it."

"What, like a prisoner?" Pickett tried to think of all the temples she'd seen in her life. The twin temples of Mother Love and Father Rain in Verran. Or maybe Tyrrane. Yes, she was pretty sure that was right. It had been cold, even when she'd been bundled in the back of her father's cart. Or maybe it had just been winter, and she'd been too young to really know where they were in any given season.

Regardless, they were all holy places people flocked to, all places that got a lot of love and care without being able to prove they did anyone any good. But none of them, to Pickett's memory, imprisoned people.

"Who locked her up?" Jodiah asked, his brows furrowing. "I'm not busting out someone who's meant to be a sacrifice."

"Al-Dagos doesn't demand sacrifices," Simon huffed. "Nancy's been forced into training to be a patroness, that being a holy virgin, by her father. He wants to ensure she lives a holy life, even if it's against her will. It'll be our job to get her out."

Pickett arched a brow. "We're meant to believe someone hired you to put a team together to free a holy virgin from a cushy temple with food and shelter and a squishy bed, and they're actually going to pay us all to do it?"

Simon beamed and spread his hands. "Exactly. Think of this as us liberating and ensuring the freedom of a lady."

Jodiah squirmed a little more in his seat, eyes widening as he shot Pickett a look. "I don't like this," he grumbled. "Crossing gods and such. This girl's a patroness to Al-Dagos. It might be best to leave her be."

Pickett rolled her eyes. "I will once again remind you that the gods have fucked off to the Untamed Paradise. What do they care if one virgin stops working for them?"

"But stealing a woman from the temple is going into their territory." Jodiah knocked back the last of his rum and went to stand.

Fuck. If he left, that was one less person Pickett could use as a shield between her and her brother. Pickett grabbed his sleeve and gave him a sharp jerk and hissed, "Where the fuck do you think you're going? We might need muscle."

At the same time, Edie smiled and captured Simon's gaze. "So tell us, why does this benefactor need help to free her?"

Simon smirked and pointed at Pickett. "That's why we need a swamp witch. Nora, surely you're clever enough to, uh, help us bypass a *srrcrrsss*." He muttered the last bit, dropping his gaze.

Heat flooded Pickett's cheeks as she shot to her feet. "What did you say?"

Simon heaved a deep breath. "Nancy is guarded by a-a-a sorceress."

Pickett might have smashed his nose anew if Edie hadn't rested a hand on Letterboy's shoulder, signaling him to rest a shoulder on Pickett's. Jodiah dropped his face into his hands and started muttering about gods and demons and other shit the pious cared about. All Pickett knew about gods was the odd temple and the swears from the patrons at the Spotted Dick brothel. She didn't know what he needed to hear to feel secure. She only knew she didn't want to be the point man on this awful job.

"And you decided a swamp witch and a bounty hunter were good enough for this? Sorry, Simon, but you aren't getting paid, because if Jodiah walks, so do I."

"Pickett," Edie hissed, but Pickett shrugged. It wasn't like this was a bluff. She was only considering the offer because Edie wanted to.

Simon groaned and scratched his chin. "Jodiah, come on. If I know my sister, I know she's scrappy."

It was true, but Pickett had to bite her tongue to stop herself from reminding him that, no, he didn't actually know her.

Jodiah began to bounce his leg. "This feels dangerous. Screwing gods and sorcerers."

"All to save an innocent young lady," Simon insisted. "Won't it be nice to complete a bounty that makes someone happy?"

"Every bounty makes someone happy," Jodiah muttered.

"And don't you think Al-Dagos is unhappy to have an unwilling patroness?" Simon shifted in his chair, eyes widening in what was probably his attempt to be convincing.

Pickett rolled her eyes and slumped in her chair.

"You assume the dragon god gives two halves of a shit about those temples," she muttered.

"Wait." Letterboy stood up on his chair and planted his hands on his hips. "How much money could we make?"

Simon drummed his fingers on the table. "Apologies, but I'm not employing a child. The fee my benefactor offered was half a sun each by the end of it. For every adult participant."

Half a sun? Half a *sun*? Was it even safe for a person to carry around that sort of money? Suddenly, Edie's dream of sitting on a pirate-infested beach, sipping fruit juices and only occasionally having to fight to defend themselves seemed far more likely and appealing. Simon's face somehow transformed into something considerably less punchable with the promise of half a sun behind it.

"This girl must be able to shit gold if your benefactor's willing to pay two whole suns to get her out," Pickett mused. "What did you say your benefactor's name was?"

Simon shrugged. "Understandably, he didn't give it. But I can assure you he has the money. He even paid for the messenger I used to contact you."

"You used a messenger because you knew I'd punch you if you walked in here," Pickett pointed out.

Simon touched his nose. "Regardless, the money will be there. I just need you to scope out how to free the girl. I'll secure a ship we can use to escape. We rendezvous in three days at the tavern where I'll set you up, at which point we can whisk Nancy off to a better life."

Pickett glanced at Jodiah. The hunter seemed a little less terrified and a little more intrigued by the sudden possibility of that sort of wealth.

"I suppose, if the girl's there against her will, then her presence could be seen as an insult to the gods."

"That's the spirit!" Simon clapped him on the shoulder then withdrew as Jodiah shot him a murderous glare.

Letterboy, grubby little urchin that he was, grinned wolfishly. "Don't worry, you'll be fine. I think you're forgetting Edie's the best person in the room for this."

Edie flushed.

"Letterboy—" she started, but Letterboy cut her off.

"She's smart, and she's nice." He glanced between them, then smacked his hand on the table. "I'm serious. She could probably just talk the holy folk into letting her in. And on top of that, she does magic too. Magic scribbles!"

Pickett pinched the bridge of her nose. "Runes."

"Scribble runes."

Jodiah leaned forward. "Edie, is that true?"

Edie shifted uneasily in her chair. "I mean, I've tried a little, but I've only just started to learn."

"A runecaster," Simon breathed. "Well I'll be damned."

Pickett reached across Letterboy to give Edie's wrist a squeeze. "You don't have to if you don't want. Just say the word and we walk." It took every ounce of the goodwill she had to say that. Half a sun. Each. Fuck, she didn't want to walk away from money like that. But for Edie . . .

Edie took a deep breath and nodded. "Let's do it."

SEVEN

After that meeting, there wasn't much time to waste. Simon left to make arrangements for lodgings and, most importantly, a ship to smuggle Nancy onto once the job was done. Jodiah would accompany him to make sure he did exactly what he said he was doing. Pickett and Edie would settle into Southfen and take three days to plot how, exactly, to bypass the sorceress so they could extract Nancy.

While Pickett fussed over just what "witchery" it was wise to pack and whether or not she'd actually use blackout bottles, Edie took off for the night to secure a little additional help running the bar while they were gone. "Help" was somewhat of an ambiguous way to put it. The last Pickett had seen of Hoag, the old swamp-man was swimming with a dragon-ish monster near the remains of his shattered houseboat. He'd looked so content. Perhaps living in the swamp would drive them all equally mad one day.

With Edie gone, that left Pickett to run the bar with their . . . Ward? Pet? What was the little urchin to them anyway?

Letterboy positively bounced off the walls in anticipation. Pickett had to check his cup to make sure he hadn't snuck a sip of rum. But no, this was just how he was, half-jogging to drop drinks off at tables, foamy beer sloshing over the edges so he'd have to return with a rag to mop it up. But that big, goofy grin never left his face. Almost a shame that Edie insisted they be responsible guardians to him. It was something Pickett never agreed to—the guardian or the responsible bit.

"The table by the window wants a whole tray of rolls," he said, hopping onto one of the stools. "One of 'em's gonna try and stand on his head and he says he needs the stamina. I think I'll really miss the shows while we're in town."

"You know you're not coming with us, right?" she asked as she spot-checked a plate before preparing the order.

Letterboy's face fell. "What? Why not?"

"Because it's dangerous and Edie says no." Pickett pushed the plate across the bar to him. "Be sure to let the customer know if he pukes this up he's going to clean it himself."

Letterboy didn't even touch it. "That's not fair! I used to be the best messenger in Southfen. You'd be a damned fool to leave me behind."

"Damned fool to take you in too." Pickett pointed at the table. "Go. Serve."

Letterboy shot her an utterly filthy look and stuffed one of the rolls defiantly into his mouth before stalking to his table with the rest. It was endearing really. Pickett hadn't had his spunk when she'd been his age, though it might have served her well. He'd be fine. To Pickett, the whole notion of him staying behind seemed silly, but Edie was so soft on him.

After the one fellow did his headstand (he didn't vomit but he did let out a ghastly fart that scared anyone from performing for a good half an hour) and two more singers went up, Edie finally returned from her errand with a guest in tow. Hoag looked very much like a torch with his red hair, brown skin, and eyes bright like embers.

"Hoag." Pickett stepped out from behind the bar, one hand

extended. But Hoag scampered past her, stooping low as he rapped his knuckles on the bar. Before she could stop him, he darted to the nearest table, shoving his hand between two bounty hunters, never mind they were armed to the teeth, and knocked on their table. And the next. And the next until there wasn't a flat surface in the bar that had escaped him.

Edie smoothed her skirt and cocked her head to the side. "Do you think he was dropped on his head as a baby or was it maybe being denied air too long?"

"Maybe something he read." Pickett shrugged. "If food can turn a stomach funny, why can't books turn a mind funny?"

"Oh, so I take my life in my hands every time I read?" Edie arched a brow, and Pickett could only grin wider.

"That's why I prefer to just listen to you read aloud. Protects my head, see?"

Edie rolled her eyes, but there was no mistaking that hint of a smile at the corner of her lips. Hoag knocked on one side of the stage, then the other, thoroughly disrupting the one-eyed bounty hunter in the middle of his juggling act, before returning to them, looking utterly pleased with himself.

"A sturdy home you have here, my lady witch," he said, bobbing his head up and down. "Sturdy and safe."

Clearly he didn't know about the old holes in the floor or the fact that, before her servitude, the place had been ready to crumble into the Rottering waters. Pickett inclined her head. "And how is your home? Hopefully no undead have come to destroy it again."

"Certainly not. The swamp is happy. It swims with hope and new possibilities. Also Muriel helped me rebuild."

"Muriel?" Edie frowned. "The swamp beast Muriel? Does she even have thumbs?"

Hoag's eyes lit up with indignation as he stamped his foot. "Do not question the great lady of the swamp! She needs no thumbs to avail herself to old friends."

"Right. Sorry." Edie cleared her throat. "Well thank you again for looking after the bar. And Letterboy."

Letterboy scowled and crossed his arms, glaring up at Hoag. "I don't need a minder," he said gloomily.

What the fuck was she supposed to say to that? When she'd been Letterboy's age, she hadn't exactly had a minder. Moreover, Letterboy had gone years running errands in Southfen before they'd taken him in. What would Edie say here?

"Maybe, but the bar does." Pickett ruffled his hair the way she saw Edie do it sometimes before she bent down and whispered in his ear. "And between you and me, Hoag does need a minder. Edie and I can't check up on him from Southfen. Can you keep him safe?"

Letterboy snorted and took a step back. "How naïve do you think I am?"

Pickett shrugged. "Worth a shot. Anyway, he'll be here with you until Edie and I get back. Don't burn the bar down. Don't give any of the customers food poisoning. Don't serve full-bodied drinks after midnight."

"Edie said to stop watering them down."

Of course she did. Pickett sighed. "Fine. Double the price on anyone who looks like they'll get rowdy and, most importantly, don't die."

Letterboy continued to scowl at her, even as Hoag slapped his forehead in what Pickett assumed was some sort of salute. This was probably a good idea. Or, at the very least, it wasn't the worst idea she and Edie had ever had. Probably.

As Pickett ducked into their room to gather their bags, Edie walked Hoag through how to run the bar then had Letterboy follow up as the person to actually remember the instructions. Between the two of them, they were leaving the Pick's Pocket in the hands of approximately one functional adult.

Edie gave Letterboy a long embrace, and the two exchanged words. Pickett didn't hear what they were saying. She didn't try to. It felt like something private. But she did give the kid a wink before shaking Hoag's hand and shouldering her bag. The bar had never been safer or more profitable. Hoag and Letterboy could be trusted. The job would take a few days at most and they'd be back home, rich as royals. Yet, even knowing it, Pickett couldn't make her feet move.

It took Edie pressing a hand to the small of her back to convince Pickett to shuffle one foot forward. Then the other, again and again until they were out of the bar and onto the boardwalks. Pickett breathed in the stinking swamp air and felt a little more awake and alert. They were used to staying up all night. So being awake and walking through the swamp wouldn't be too different from staying awake and serving customers. She could just focus on that and not on what lay ahead or behind.

"Don't be so grim," Edie said, nudging Pickett a little. "This is a good thing, remember?"

"Right. Good." Pickett sighed and breathed in the fetid smell of the Rottering swamp. Home. It felt like she'd only just come home and now she had to leave again. "Give us a song if you want the trip to be pleasant."

Edie smiled and began humming then switched to singing. She hit a pitch like a backwards, blindfolded archer, but it still made Pickett feel warm when she started.

> "My mother told a story
> Of a man who loved a mare.
> But in a feeble human form,
> He could not love declare.
>
> So off he went to see a demon
> Foul as 'ere was born,
> So that he might be afterwards
> Into a horse transformed."

Pickett laughed and hummed along as they slowly but steadily made their way along the boardwalks to land. Maybe a horse wouldn't be a bad idea. She didn't know how the hell they'd keep it, and maybe it wouldn't make the trip to Southfen faster, but at least they could save their legs. Weirdly, she couldn't help but wonder if Letterboy might like having an animal to look after. She'd liked animals when she was his age. At least, she was pretty sure she did. It had been a while ago. And of course there'd be shit to muck, which Picket had endured enough of in the Elowey stables. If they ever got any sort of animal, she'd make sure it was on the kid to clean up after it.

Shit. Was she going to miss him? No, she was just going to miss the bar. Letterboy was like an extra sprout in a potato garden.

"Come on," Edie said. "You need to entertain me too. Let's both of us have the next verse."

Well, if she had to.

> "His hands and feet to hooves were turned.
> His nose grew long and wide.
> And off he went, his tail a-swish
> Unto his horsey bride.
>
> But when he came home to the farm,
> He learned to his dismay
> His human wife did sell her off
> To save on feed and hay."

CHAPTER

EIGHT

I t was just a little after dawn, the time when at least one of them would be in bed, when they finally reached land. The morning birds and frogs darted through bits where the water met the land, forming a thick stew of mud and grass. It stank a little less than the swamp proper, but that didn't say much.

"I thought it would smell good out here," Edie said with a frown. "Strange. It's not much better. I wonder how many of the undead from the incident rotted close to . . ." Her expression fell. "Oh no."

Pickett's stomach dropped. Someone had fixed the sign announcing the road and, beyond it, the trees were already being felled. It looked like a gash in the woods. A gash that would turn into a road that would drive away business.

"Will even the bounty hunters come by when there's an easier path to Southfen and all the shitty villages?"

Edie wrapped her arm around Pickett's shoulder and gave her a squeeze.

"They'd never leave," she insisted. "They love our bar. In

fact, we're building a reputation so strong, people will brave the stench to visit us. Even when they don't have to."

"And if whoever's running Sedrios decides to stop having the boardwalks rebuilt because of it?"

"Then we'll have plenty of money from this job to maintain them all by ourselves."

Pickett smiled and patted Edie's hand. For the moment, she chose to believe that. Maybe it would have been easier if circumstances were different, but Simon's reappearance in her life had fucked up what little peace they'd had. If this didn't work out, she was going to gut him.

Pickett stifled a yawn. "All right. Come on. The sooner we get to town, the sooner we can catch a few winks of sleep. But keep your bag under the pillow when we get there."

"I'm prepared." Edie winked. "Even if the people in Gall-raven didn't tend to steal, the goats did. I got clever with what I had. And what kind of pirate is as bad as a goat?"

"They're not pirates. Just pirate adjacent. Culturally influenced. They don't become pirates until they board a ship and steal shit."

"I wonder if it's a coming of age for growing pirate babies," Edie mused. "Not a man or woman until you steal a ship and plunder something."

Now that was an image Pickett had to smile at.

They made their way down the dirt road and trees not yet sacrificed to the building of the new road until, at last, they passed through into the city proper. Funny. It still looked the same. She'd been just a girl the first time she stepped into this place. Maybe it was because Edie was looking at it with bright eyes but, somehow, every time since then faded away and all she could think of was that first, before she grew up, before she lived life. Her gut squirmed at the memory.

Though still with her father and brother, it had been two days since she'd eaten and she hadn't really grasped what was happening. All she knew was that an orven had come to croak out something only her father heard. Next thing she knew, her father'd disappeared. At that time, Pickett hadn't understood how expensive it could be to send an orven. She certainly hadn't realized that it meant someone very powerful and very wealthy was very angry with him. Simon understood, though, and he'd made the decision to drive the cart away. They'd sold the remainder of their father's wares. They'd sold the pans and their shoes. They'd sold their blankets and their mule and the cart, but the money never lasted long enough. She'd been so small and skinny and so hungry, it felt like there was a hole inside of her. More than that, she'd felt like more hole than person.

"Trust me," Simon had whispered. *"In Southfen, everything will be different. Everything will be better."*

The fucker.

Southfen wasn't supposed to hurt like that, but Simon coming back into her life felt like cutting open a tender scar again, just so it could bleed. Pickett wanted to take Edie's hand, cling to her arm, let Edie keep her safe for a little while. But she wasn't going to do that. Edie was too busy enjoying herself.

"They're so tall," Edie breathed, not one bit ashamed to point at the three, even four-story buildings that towered over them. "Nobody built anything so tall in Gallraven."

"That's because you come from a shithole village," Pickett pointed out. "Anyway, half of them are leaning on each other. If one were to burn, half the street would collapse."

"And the road." Edie laughed as she kicked the ground. "It's half dirt, half cobblestone."

"It's lazy craftsmanship."

"And the cobblestones change from street to street."

"It's not as though they planned and built all of Southfen at once."

Pickett frowned and glanced around. Southfen was a conundrum, that was for certain. There were more beggars than she remembered, huddling under the meager shade of stoops, their arms outstretched. But there were also more fruit stands and peddlers hawking fine silks and jewels. Rich and poor, Southfen stretched both ways.

Edie began to zip back and forth, examining food stalls and sniffing the traveler's rolls, fresh fruit, and spices on display for sale. Pickett would have to rein her in once they got further down the street and passed by the brothels—particularly the Spotted Dick. Even from where she was, she could make out the whitewash of its exterior, gleaming in the sun. Her heart skipped a beat at how different it looked. She'd once stood on this street with Simon, hungry and desperate. The place had been yellow back then, one of many shades it would be painted over the years.

The first time she'd walked these streets, it had been hand in hand with Simon.

"Come on," he'd said over and over. *"Surely the next one will take in a little girl."*

Which, to Pickett's child brain, had been an insult. She hadn't thought of herself as little at the time. She'd been so young.

Four places had turned them down. The fifth had a man with rotted teeth who wanted to buy her.

Edie didn't see all of that, though. She saw a booming city full of wonders her shitty little village never could have provided. Just seeing her wide eyes and smile made Pickett smile too. Just a little.

"Hey." She nudged Edie and pointed at the building. "That's where I grew up."

Edie glanced over and frowned. "The Spotted Dick?"

"It's actually a reputable establishment. And the woman who took me in was . . . She was kind."

Edie said nothing to that, but her smile slipped just a bit. She slid her hand into Pickett's and gave it a squeeze that pushed Pickett's heart right up into her throat.

Fuck.

Fuck Simon for coming back. Fuck him for abandoning her. Fuck this job. Once she and Edie had a whole sun between them, they'd be rich enough to do whatever they wanted and she'd never have to remember anything she disliked ever again. Wealthy people got to float about in a happy haze until they choked on their own fine food. That would be the life.

The balcony door opened.

A woman stepped out.

Even though there were more lines on her face, she still wore her hair in those elegant loops. She still carried herself like a goddess. To the randy sailors who docked here, she might have been. She was, after all, the Madame of the Spotted Dick. Tears sprang to Pickett's eyes and she turned, hiding her face behind her mane of hair. Why the fuck was Merca still working at that place? Surely she could have retired years ago.

"Edie," she called, "I think we should hurry along to the inn. Now."

"What?" Edie glanced over her shoulder, an orange in each hand. The vendor eyed her warily, no doubt ready to wallop her if she took even a step in the wrong direction without paying. "The room won't be ready until midday."

"I just—"

Hooves clopped on the uneven stones. Crowds parted. Anyone who could afford a carriage in Southfen could afford not to pay damages if they ran a person over. Pickett jumped out of the way, as a carriage rumbled toward them then stopped right in front of her.

On the door was Fistic's symbol, a painted schooner with three coins above it. The richest moneylender in Southfen had found her already. Fucking perfect.

The door swung open and a handsome man leaned forward, his expression carefully neutral and pleasant.

"Pickett, lovely to see you." He gestured at the cab with his cane. "Come in. I'd love to have a word."

Pickett glanced back at Edie, who'd squeezed one of the oranges so tight that juice dribbled down her fingers. She ignored the vendor yelling at her, completely focused on Pickett as she was.

Fistic waved a hand. "Oh I'll have one of my friends look after her. Make sure she gets where she's going. But I could use a word with you."

"Sorry, *friend*, but I recall our relationship being transactional." Pickett jerked a thumb over her shoulder. "Since Edie bought out the rest of my contract, you and I are more or less through with our business."

"Indeed." Fistic rummaged with something in the carriage then tossed a small pouch out of the open window. It hit the ground with the unmistakable clank of coins.

Edie bristled. "You think you can just buy us?" she demanded.

"Only her," Fistic explained, gesturing to Pickett. "Between the coin and my knowledge of certain missing ornaments, I should say I've successfully purchased a short carriage ride. What say you, friend?"

Pickett could feel the eyes on her from the vendor, from Edie, from the people on the street, and from the balcony of the Spotted Dick. The pack on her shoulder felt twice as heavy, weighed down by the stolen comb. Fuck, how did he know about it?

She cleared her throat and forced a smile. "Always happy to catch up. Edie, I'll meet you at the inn."

"Pickett?"

Pickett glanced over her shoulder. "I'll be fine. Just go straight there. Don't stop for anyone. I'm certain I'll be right behind you."

"Splendid," Fistic said, and he swung open the door.

CHAPTER

NINE

Pickett had never been inside of a private carriage before. It moved more smoothly than the back of somebody's cart, and the cushion under her bottom spared her any unwanted jolts from the uneven streets of Southfen. The interior, likewise, was exactly what she'd expected from Fistic. The walls were covered with an ornate, turquoise paper decorated with birds and vines and flowers. The seats had velvet cushions on them. During a long day of not walking, surely one needed a nice place to rest one's ass. Even the air smelled just a bit perfumed, which was impressive given the cage hanging from the ceiling between them, with a live tropical bird inside. Across from her was the man himself.

Hurb Fistic was certainly nothing if not handsome, heavy in a very well-fed but not overindulgent sort of way. There was something about him that made a person want his approval. It was probably what made him so good at wringing coins out of poor borrowers.

Pickett leaned back in her seat. Fuck, even the inside of the doors had cushions. Was Fistic afraid of knocking his knees on them when he got in and out of the carriage? It took everything she had not to poke at them, just to assure herself they were real.

"My old friend," Fistic said, fixing his hungry eyes on her. They were the only unattractive part of him. Being caught in that gaze always made Pickett want to go still, like a deer hoping to hide in the brush from a hunter.

She rested one hand on her day pack and leaned back, stretching across the narrow floor. "Friends, are we? What's a little unpaid debt between friends?"

"Indeed. And on that note, what's a little indentured servitude between friends?" He laced his fingers together and rested them on his brocade waistcoat.

Fuck! Pickett had to work very, very hard not to hug the bag to her chest. He didn't look angry about the comb. In fact, there was a twinkle in his dark eyes.

"The Eloweys paid me for your services, so I consider your debt to me resolved. More than, since I understand your kitchen girl got you out early. I never imagined the bar would be so profitable."

"Well Edie knows how to attract business."

The bird in the cage between them began to squawk, flapping his wings until Fistic pulled a seed from his waistcoat pocket and held it up to the bars. The bird snatched it from his fingers and crunched.

"Mm. And your enchantments couldn't do that?" Fistic purred

"Hard to enchant from the Elowey estate."

This time, Fistic grinned wide enough to show his teeth. "My dear swamp witch, even when I doubt you, you do manage to please me. I would like to take this moment to thank you for your service to the dear Eloweys. I understand you were exactly the sort of quality servant I should have liked for my dear friends. And you eased them of the burden of a treasure." His hungry eyes twinkled. "You can keep it, by the way. Consider it a bonus for having to share a room with the lady of that house."

So he knew she was shit at the job and he hated the Eloweys. Pickett couldn't help grinning at that, though she didn't remove her hand from the bag. Best not to be too obvious if she wanted to keep the comb.

"So glad to help. You must have really loved them if you chose them specifically to sell such a short contract to. Is that why you've come to visit? Want me to ruffle some more feathers? I can snap fire into existence with a little warning. Heat up some of their fancy balls."

Fistic waved a hand through the air. "No, no, nothing of the sort. I had my fun, and you paid your debt. But I do know the future profitability of the Pick's Pocket is uncertain."

Pickett's smile fell into the controlled, neutral look she usually reserved for the man. "I couldn't possibly turn to you for financial aid. Not now that you and I are finally square. What kind of a friend would I be?"

"A good one, I hope."

Fistic leaned forward, dropping his hands to his knees. This close, she was able to catch a fresh whiff of the perfume filling the carriage. Tits and teeth, it was in his perfectly coiffed hair.

"Tell me," he said in a low voice. "Have you heard of the Gilt King?"

Pickett blinked. "The Gilt . . .?"

"King. Yes. Ridiculous name but apt. Some upstart new to moneylending and investment has been cutting into my business. He's purchased a number of reputable and disreputable establishments in the town. Some have even improved. And yet the only name any of them can offer when I investigate is that ridiculous title."

"Ah. So it's not a ball you'd like me to light on fire."

Fistic wrinkled his nose. "Sadly, much as I would like you to creatively deal with my competitor, there's a reason we have to use the title. Nobody knows who he is or where he is. But if he keeps on going, we might very well have a war of commerce on our hands. Bad for business. Bad for Southfen."

"I'm not from Southfen."

"Yes, but plenty of business from this town goes into the Rottering swamp. I understand a certain guild has taken your bar as their hub of operations." Fistic arched a brow. "If money dries up, it dries up for everyone. Even bounty hunters need money. Without it, they can't buy your beer."

"Then I'm certain they'll find work in the villages."

Something shone through his eyes and Pickett wanted only to slump back in her seat, but there was nowhere else to slump.

"Mm. The villages," Fistic hummed. "The new road will make it easier for them to access those. No need to cut across those rotting boardwalks when there's a stable, easy-to-maintain road. I'll even bet it won't reek of dead fish."

Pickett bit the inside of her cheek. "Maybe. Or maybe we'll be so popular they'll keep coming."

Fistic smirked. "My dear friend witch, the last time you bet on hope, you needed a madman to die and leave you his savings, and still you earned an indenture. Clearly, divination is not your strong suit."

She really hated talking to Fistic. She thought she hated talking to Jodiah, but no. He was just cocky and annoying. Fistic was smug and dangerous. Pickett clenched her jaw but forced herself to smile.

"So if I find out who the Gilt King is, you stop the road?"

Smug and dangerous, Fistic chuckled and leaned back in his seat. "That would suggest I have business dealings in the road. I don't. But the Gilt King does. Find out who he is and I'll be able to take control of the whole project. Not only can I ensure it veers toward entries into the Rottering swamp, I can convince powerful friends that we should increase funds toward the maintenance of the boardwalks. Take some of the financial pressure off a dear friend's back."

Damn. That did sound pretty good. It would certainly ensure Edie's hard work didn't go to waste. If she could keep the bounty hunters coming? Pickett hadn't even had to fake magic once since they'd taken up residence. But a deal with Fistic . . .

"And if I fail to discover the Gilt King's identity?" she asked airily. "What will become of you?"

Fistic shrugged. "I've already secured the assets most important to me. I would just hate to let an opportunity this tempting pass us both by. Mutual gain if you succeed. Nothing lost if you don't."

The carriage rolled to a stop. Fistic held out his hand. Pickett eyed it for a long moment before she rose, gripping her bag tightly.

"I'll let you know if I find anything," she said. "I have no doubt you've got ears all over the city. You won't be hard to find."

Fistic grinned and leaned back in his seat. "A pleasure as always, my lady witch."

TEN

Pickett stumbled right out of the carriage and onto the stoop of the hotel Simon had arranged for them. The Fair Fishman of Southfen looked like any brothel on the street but with a slightly different smell. How Fistic knew where they were staying, Pickett couldn't tell. But he couldn't be omniscient. If he was, he'd never have called upon her to sniff out the Gilt King's identity.

Pickett forced herself not to glance back over her shoulder as she headed into the Fair Fishman.

The interior was about as she'd expected. The front had wide windows, but they had plenty of lanterns burning in addition to a hearth which gave the whole room a sweaty, sweltering feeling. In the hearth was a massive cauldron, no doubt the source of the spicy smell filling the air. Places like this always had a perpetual stew going for weeks, even months on end if they could keep the fire going. Her stomach gave a soft rumble at the sight, but Pickett bit her cheek and turned away. There would be time for food later.

At the wide bar stood a burly man scratching the prices onto a chalkboard. Under a rather crude picture of a fish, it listed the daily special, which was stew. So it probably wasn't so much a daily special as the only special he ever offered. He had no hair on the top of his head, but Pickett wouldn't go so far as to call him hairless, since it looked like most of it had migrated down to his very large and very bushy beard.

"I understand I have a room waiting for me," Pickett said, leaning on the counter.

The man must have been growing displaced hair in his ears too because he didn't respond. Pickett scowled and flicked her wrist, slipping her flint rings onto her knuckles. As she snapped, a bright, blue spark shot through the air.

The bar man jumped back, his wooden mug clattering to the floor. Pickett smiled just a little wickedly. She hadn't had to do that in a while. Good to know she still had the magic touch.

"I understand a room is waiting for the swamp witch."

"Oh. Right. Yes," he spluttered, ducking down under the counter until she couldn't see even one of his misplaced hairs, which was impressive. There was a lot of him to hide. When he re-emerged, it was with both his wooden mug and a brass key.

"Second floor. Your patron requested the blue room."

"Um, all right." Pickett took the key. "And what number is the blue room?"

He shrugged and resumed his polishing of the mug. "You'll know it when you see it."

Right. Pickett adjusted the strap of her pack and headed up the rickety stairs, each one creaking in a slightly different pitch. She would bet good money that this was an intentional way of keeping an ear out for people creeping around after dark.

As she climbed onto the second floor landing, half a dozen doors stretched out in front of her. Each one had a carving of a nude man with a literal fish for a head, each fish painted a different color. Pickett had to stare for a moment. Maybe whomever was responsible for the décor here had a weird sense of humor. Or else, they wanted to make their nightmares into everybody's problem.

Pickett tried to avoid looking too closely at the crude carvings as she tracked down the blue-headed abomination at the end of the hall.

She barely had time to insert and twist the key, before the door flew open and Edie hurled herself at Pickett, wrapping her in a tight hug.

"Are you all right? What did he want?" She pulled back and inspected Pickett all over, presumably for injuries. As far as Pickett knew, Edie wouldn't know how to treat anything worse than a sliced thumb anyway.

She smiled and caught her hand. "I'm fine. Fistic's trying to get me to help him with a business matter."

Edie frowned. "And you told him no."

"I told him maybe. If it looks worthwhile."

"Pickett, the man sold you into servitude."

Pickett grinned and shrugged. "Like I said, we'll see. So this is our room?"

Edie lit up and nodded. She positively scampered back through the door, gesturing widely at their accommodations. The room wasn't huge, exactly, but it was easily twice the size of the oversized closet they slept in back home. There was a chest of drawers, a dingy mirror and washbasin, and even a little table next to the window. And one bed. Pickett had to force herself not to stare too hard at that as she made her way to the open window. The hinges on the shutters were rusted, and she was pretty sure if they opened or closed too quickly, that would be that. But this room had the most important thing: a clear view of the temple of Al Dagos.

"So that's the place, huh?"

"I managed to check without the moneylender's man catching on to what I was doing," Edie said, leaning against the wall next to Pickett.

Somehow, Pickett imagined a temple would look nicer. Sure, it had iron fences around it, quite the commodity in Southfen. They probably had to paint them that shade of black regularly to protect the metal from the corrosive sea breeze. But within the gate? It looked just like any other building in Southfen. It might have been a little bigger with its two floors and a gap in the roof that suggested it had some sort of interior courtyard. But beyond that, it looked to be a ramshackle building of wood and stone, probably thrown together and repaired again and again over the years.

"Well we can't accuse Al Dagos of being the wealthiest of gods," Pickett muttered. "Then again, what do gods care for money or assholes on the continent asking for attention they're not going to get?"

"I hear their holy people care quite a lot," Edie said. "Wulf said it's not unheard of for the odd devotee to rough up strangers when they need money."

"Wulf?"

"The barman." Edie pointed to the door. "Big. Hairy except for the top of his head?"

"He told you his name?" Pickett wrinkled her nose. "He wouldn't even acknowledge me."

Edie planted her hands on her hips. "Were you friendly?"

"I'm always friendly." Pickett plopped down in one of the table chairs and leaned forward. "So. Do we just keep watch?"

"Your brother hasn't given us anything else to do, for now, and this feels like the way to spend day one." Edie sank down opposite her and dug something out of her pocket. It looked like a parchment folded over and again a half dozen times.

"Is that your rune pamphlet?"

Edie nodded and held it up. It had all sorts of strange, foreign symbols scribbled on it with the odd note here and there to define them: *protection, fire, storm,* and *summon.*

Pickett leaned forward to tug the corner of the pamphlet, but she didn't pull it from Edie's grasp. "And who gave this to you? The bar's new investor?"

"Bresk, yes." Edie smoothed the paper down on the table and arched a brow. "Are you taking an interest?"

"In whatever idiot wants to give us money? Sure." Pickett sucked her teeth, then chewed the inside of her lip. She didn't know anything about runes or any of this, but surely information on them was valuable. What interest would a stranger have in them that he'd not only give it up but invest in the Pick's Pocket? "This Bresk didn't mention . . . You didn't hear anything about a Gilt King did you?"

"Gilt King?" Edie blinked slowly, then snorted. "Who's going around calling himself the Gilt King?"

"Some idiot. Just wondering if he's *your* idiot."

"*Our* idiot," Edie corrected. "Someday, you'll meet him and you'll see. Bresk is a sound investor. And between him and what we make from this job, we'll be set for life."

"One can only hope," Pickett grumbled. "Fistic's asked me to keep an eye out for a potential rival in the city. He wants me to find out the Gilt King's real identity. That has me thinking about the miraculous investor who's coming in and helping out an old swamp bar that used to be Fistic's investment."

Edie arched a brow. "You think Bresk is the Gilt King?

"I feel like if your Bresk worked for Fistic, the man himself would have bragged about how he's keeping us afloat. Instead, he paid us. Bresk doesn't work for Fistic."

Edie rolled her eyes. "There's no need for cynicism. Someone can make a business investment without some grand plan."

"It's not cynicism, Edie; it's practicality. I will bet you a week's worth of kitchen cleaning that he's the Gilt King."

"And I will bet the same that he isn't," Edie said primly.

Pickett smirked as she rested a cheek on her hand and gazed out the open window at the temple.

WATCHING a half-corrupt temple on the job of a lifetime was not, as it turned out, particularly exciting. Traffic moved belowon the street. At one point, a woman with a veil and a scaled leather pauldron on one arm left the temple, but she returned not long after with a wheel of cheese and what appeared to be a bag bulging with bread.

"Do you think we could try freeing the girl during one of their grocery runs?" Pickett asked dully.

Edie grunted but didn't glance up from her task. Pickett hadn't watched too closely, but she had caught sight of Edie drawing multiple runes at a time on the table with her finger over and over. If she kept at it much longer, she'd wear her finger raw.

"What are you doing?"

Edie jabbed a finger at the pamphlet. "It's not a lot of runes. I gather there are a lot more. But there are some for protection. Some for shielding. Some for safety. Then for other things. Fire. Water. I want to see what happens when I mix them together."

"So you're drawing magic?"

"No. It's more . . ." Edie bit her lip and furrowed her brows. "I suppose I can describe it a bit like cooking. We agree my pocket rolls are delicious."

"Fucking delicious," Pickett said. "I dunno how we ever operated without them."

"Well they're made of a bunch of things. Flour and water and fish and the like. Alone they're fine, but they're not pocket rolls. And I, for one, wouldn't have much use for plain flour. But you mix them together and add a touch of heat and you get what you want. The runes are like that."

Pickett hummed and turned back to the window. Someone passed by with a hefty box of salted fish, walking a little too slowly to be natural. It was confirmed by his hawking calls.

"Salty. Fishy. Good for the ladies and the lads!"

Fuck. Now she was hungry too.

Edie continued to draw with the runes on the table until the smell of burning wood filled the air. Edie shrieked and jumped back. Pickett slammed her hand over the flame.

"That's enough experimentation," she said. "I think Nancy's going to be locked up for the night. Have you ever had a vacation, Edie?"

Edie narrowed her eyes. "Not many opportunities to relax and stop work in Gallraven or the swamp."

Pickett jerked a thumb at the door. "Here's your chance. It feels like nothing else to do tonight. My pigshit brother has the room and probably the tab too."

"Pickett, should we really take advantage?"

"Of course." Pickett grinned. "If he's as wealthy as he says, he can afford the bar tab. Fuck's sake, he's got money to charter a ship just to get this girl out of here. Once he shows up with it, we're back to work. For tonight, we're off. Let's go downstairs and pretend we're on vacation."

The Fair Fishman, like any place with a bar, appeared to operate more or less the same as the Pick's Pocket. It was quiet and dedicated only to day-to-day operations while the sun was up, but the moment the sky began to darken, people flocked to the most convenient booze-slinging joint. But this one, at least, had a perpetual stew. It probably made up for the fact that the Fair Fishman, unlike so many other establishments on this side of Southfen, had no ladies or lads of the night.

Pickett felt strange, as if she was herself and not, as she sat at the bar rather than behind it.

"Can we have a menu?" Edie asked brightly.

Pickett wrinkled her nose. "Menu? What kind of place do you think this is?"

And yet hairy, hairless Wulf grunted and handed her a scrappy pamphlet that made Edie's folded-up rune sheet look fine and polished. As Edie spread it out over the counter, Pickett had to bite her tongue.

"This all looks lovely," Edie breathed. "And you serve all this every day?"

"Every day except when the trading ships are late. But they usually ain't." Wulf shrugged. "Even the pirates know some shit's gotta show up on time if they want their fucking shore leave."

Edie ran her finger down the menu. "We want to have a night of it so maybe some bread. A bowl of stew. Seasonal vegetables, I think. Honey bread. And perhaps"—she pursed her lips—"the Ocean's Breath and the Eel's Cock."

As Wulf took the menu back, Pickett leaned over. "Since when do you have such rich taste?"

"Since your bother was footing the bill."

Pickett grinned and nodded. "Well I won't be the one drinking the Eel's Cock."

The stew came. It was stew. Better salted than what Edie could usually make, maybe. And fattier. That had Pickett lapping up the sides of the bowls with her bread. But it was the drinks that clearly made this place special.

"Fuck," she hissed, as the first swallow went down. It was rum, yes. But whatever bright, fruity something they'd added to it was leagues beyond the cheap bibblewood juice they used in the Pick's Pocket. Edie, meanwhile, savored the Eel's Cock. Despite herself, Pickett had to try that too. Briney but not like gulping seawater.

"Is that olive?" she asked, smacking her lips.

"I don't know, but I like it," Edie declared. "Pickett, we have to figure out how to start making drinks like this."

Why not? When this job was over, they'd have a whole sun between them. They'd be able to afford the very best ingredients.

"Wulf!" she called. "We'd like to try all these special drinks of yours. Put it on the room tab."

If this was what vacation was, then fuck yes. They needed to do this every year. Preferably with her brother picking up the tab but without having to talk to him.

They tried the Stormy Cloud, the Demon's Eye, the Dragon's Tooth, the Sailor's Fortune, and the Muddy Harbor. They sampled the traveler's buns and hard, black bittersweets molded into the shape of tiny fish. Pickett had to stop herself from laughing as Edie spat hers out, her whole face twisted in revulsion.

"Why would you call those sweets?" she demanded. "They aren't sweet at all?"

Pickett only laughed and helped herself to the whole small bowl. The treats had more burn and spice to them than sweetness, but they'd been her favorite during those years of working in the Spotted Dick.

After the second drink, Edie began to relax, lazily tracing her finger over the counter, still practicing her runes. Pickett would just have to watch to make sure another fire didn't erupt, made all the more difficult when Edie nicked one of Wulf's sticks of chalk from behind the bar and began drawing onto the wood, only to wipe it out. Maybe it was just the final haze of the cocktails coming over her, but Pickett didn't feel too worried about it.

"We could save a fortune on tricks to keep the mystery up," she mused. "Though you'll have to replace me as swamp witch."

"Me? Never." Edie grinned and continued to play with the chalk.

"And you're sure this stuff is safe?" she asked. "I mean, what do we really know about Bresk?"

"About as much as we know about Fistic," Edie pointed out. "And you're willing to work with him if the opportunity presents itself."

"That's different. I know to look for a knife if it comes from him," Pickett muttered. "Fistic's been my moneylender for years. He's one of the best-known names in Southfen. Bresk is nobody. You're going to be cleaning the kitchen alone when I win this bet because you're so trusting, Edie. Why are you so trusting?"

Edie smiled at her, looking utterly blissful in a way she never did back home.

"Because trusting you worked out pretty well for me." She sketched a little circle of runes onto the counter, then touched it with the very tip of her nail. Pickett had to swallow a gasp as Edie moved her hand and the chalk runes actually traveled with it, moving like a shadow over every scratch and grain in the wood. As Edie's finger danced up onto Pickett's knuckle, the runes followed, settling themselves until they were right under her middle nail.

"Edie," Pickett breathed. "This is—"

"It's for protection," Edie explained. "Same one I stitched over and over onto your new cape. I didn't want to lose you again. So don't wash that off until we're back in the room."

Suddenly, there was something caught in Pickett's throat, like a lime or a whole damn cannonball. Edie wanted to protect her. Edie wanted to keep her safe. This felt like exactly the moment to give her the comb she'd pinched from the Elowey estate. But if she went up there for it now, would that look like she just wanted to go and wash the rune off? Pickett was ready to have the thing tattooed onto her skin if anyone was available with some ink and a hot needle. Her eyes stung. Shit. Was she crying? No, but if she didn't get a hold of herself she might start.

"Maybe we shouldn't have had the whole special drink menu," Pickett croaked. "What do you say we finish our bread and head up to the—"

"'Scuse me, are you the witch?" asked a gruff voice.

Pickett turned in her seat to see a man dressed all in rough-looking linen clutching a woven reed hat to his chest. He shifted from foot to foot, glancing up at her, then down, then everywhere else before he stole another glance. Before Pickett could tell him to leave her alone, Edie popped in.

"She certainly is."

"Ah. Right." The man shifted again and cleared his throat. "Thing is, you gave my friend a charm. A stone of hidden power."

Oh. Right. The fisherman who'd taken her back to the bar.

"Look, unlocked power can't be guaranteed. If nothing happened for him—"

"No! No, miss, you see, he sold his whole cart the next day. All in one go. And I thought, well, if I could have as much luck fishing as he did trading. I-I know folks say folks like you are really demons and all, but I've just got to . . . Anyway, I've got coin to pay, miss."

One by one, other heads rose or turned to eye her cautiously. Pickett could always brush him off. Claim the alignments weren't in the air or some such. But there was coin to be had. And she couldn't help it. She fumbled around for something until Edie slipped the chalk into her palm. Pickett gave her a little smirk before she closed her eyes and pretended to focus on it.

The fisherman shuffled his feet against the floor again, and there came a snort of a near giggle from Edie next to her. Pickett would have elbowed her if it didn't give the ruse away. After about half a minute, she opened her eyes and held out the chalk.

"Write what you want on the bottom of your boat, then bury the chalk in the sand. If the sea likes what you asked, maybe you get a good catch."

The man whistled quietly, then frowned. "Wait. So the sea can listen to me? Like a god?"

"Why not." She shoved the chalk into his palm then held out her own.

He dropped a few pips into her hand, staring down at the chalk like it was carved from gemstone before frowning. "Only-only I can't write, miss. Or read."

"Then just draw pictures of fish all over the place. Make it really clear what you want."

A wide smile split his face, and he nodded feverishly. "Yes, miss. Thanks, miss."

He bobbed into an awkward bow or curtsy before scampering out. But before Pickett could turn back to the bar, a few others rose from their seats, eyeing her with equal parts suspicion and eagerness. All of them had something of value in their hands.

Edie squeezed her shoulder. "I'm going to go sleep this off. Need to be fresh in the morning."

And with that, she disappeared back up the stairs and Pickett turned back to the gathering crowd. Funny. The whole swamp witch thing had been designed to encourage people to leave her alone. It wasn't supposed to make them seek her out. Edie was rubbing off in the most congenial and unhelpful ways.

With a sigh, Pickett gestured to the first person in the line. "All right. What can the swamp witch do for you?"

When she trudged up to the room past midnight, Edie was out cold. Pickett sighed and stuffed the comb somewhere safe before flopping down onto her half of the bed.

ELEVEN

There was only so much they could accomplish by watching what appeared to be the only way in or out of the temple. After they woke up and washed up, then gulped a jug of water and a helping of rolls for the lingering hangover. It was time to work.

"According to what I've read, it's common to veil yourself in the hall of worship, or at least wear something that partially obscures your face, but only within," Edie explained as she pinned up her hair. "Something about removing all distraction from the wisdom of Al-Dagos. Outside of the hall, you have to at least show your face."

"So they can tell if assholes like us are trying to sneak in," Pickett said.

Edie nodded. "Exactly. I doubt I'll be able to make contact, but at least I'll get to scope the place. With any luck, we'll find another way out."

Pickett didn't love the idea of Edie going in there alone, but it was, for all intents and purposes, just to pray. Even the strictest of holy people couldn't possibly mind that. Of the two of them, Edie was the one who actually went out of her way to read and learn things. She'd blend in better.

They left the inn half an hour apart, with Pickett settling on the dirt with three borrowed cups and a stone. If anyone asked, she was just a street performer eager to cheat them out of their coin with the oldest game in the book while Edie headed toward the temple, a veil in the form of a tattered old skirt draped over her head.

People worked hard to avoid looking at Pickett, even going so far as to stagger a ways away from her, so she couldn't try to catch their eye and goad them into losing money on her cups—especially once she started tossing the stone from hand to hand.

When a young urchin approached her, Pickett held out her hand and shook the stone. "Care to test your luck, child?"

The boy scratched his tangled mop of hair with an intensity that made Pickett suspect he had fleas, like a dirtier version of Letterboy. Fuck. Did she miss Letterboy? No, of course not. He was Edie's pet. Pickett just got used to him. And yet, she thought she'd give a silver scale to know how he and Hoag were doing without her.

Well, shit.

The urchin plucked something out of his hair and flung it away with a sniff. "You got work?"

"What?"

"Work." He shrugged. "Deliver shit. Carry luggage. I'll work for a pip."

Pickett was prepared to tell the kid to piss off, but a thought occurred to her. "All right. Maybe for some information."

The urchin grinned and began scratching the inside of his ear with his pinkie finger. "Sure. I know things."

"Know things about kings?" Pickett asked. "Gilt kings?"

The boy paused, finger still stuck firmly in his ear. "You working for someone?"

Pickett pulled a pip from her pocket and held it up. "Does it matter?"

Quick as a frog snapping at a fly, the urchin snatched up the coin and shoved it in his dirty pocket.

"Gilt King's buying up half the city. Nobody knows much what he's planning, but we know where he started."

"And that would be?"

The kid jerked his thumb behind him. "The Spotted Dick. The last owner was running it into the ground. I think he was pretty glad to sell it off. These days, it's the nicest joint on the street."

Of course the Spotted Dick was one of the places this Gilt King person had purchased. That place was following her around just like her brother. Why the fuck was her past haunting her now?

It just made her want to break Simon's nose all the more. It would serve him right. Of course, Edie probably wouldn't let her break his nose, but Edie didn't know what it was like to be a starving kid, taken in by kind and beautiful ladies. Edie hadn't been given a meal and a safe place to live with her brother.

Edie hadn't woken up to find that brother gone. She hadn't run out onto the balcony to see him halfway down the street, a pack slung over his shoulder. It had happened so many years ago. She'd had time since then to build a new life, burn it to the ground, then the one after that for good measure. Things were good now. She had Edie. She had the bar. She even had Letter-boy, sort of. Life was good. Pickett hoped whatever ship Simon rented was a leaky one with a long drop to the ocean.

This anger swirling around her heart didn't belong. Maybe if she got around to telling Edie exactly how Simon went about ditching her, they could throw him overboard together after the job. Simon needed to get the ship and they needed to get the girl onto it if any of them wanted to make any money at all.

She tossed the kid another pip and rose to storm off somewhere, anywhere that wasn't here. She needed space to clear her mind and shake this off.

She took two steps forward when out of the corner of her eye, she spotted three men wearing vests emblazoned with the Elowey crest.

"That's her!" Spidernose snapped.

Fuck! Of all the streets in Southfen to be on in this moment. She needed to get rid of the comb, maybe duck into the inn, drop it in someone's drink or hide it behind a barrel. She patted her pockets but . . . Fuck inside a lousy fuck! It wasn't on her. Was it in the room? She shouldn't have had so many drinks.

Not that there was time to figure the situation out. The Elowey servants took a step toward her, and Pickett bolted.

Shouts came from behind as Pickett raced through the streets, narrowly dodging a fishmonger before veering dangerously close to a fruit stand. All she had to do was knock over the stand. It might slow the Elowey servants down enough to buy her time to hide somewhere. She reached out her arm to pull on the rickety wooden support but hesitated. It was one thing to nick a hair comb from a rich asshole. It was something else to fuck over a fruit seller.

But surely they could spare an orange.

She snatched a fruit, turning just enough to hurl it at the pursuers. It smacked one of the servants square in the nose. He swore and stumbled back. Damn. She'd been aiming for Spidernose.

A second too late, Pickett turned back to face an elderly man shuffling across the street, leading an equally elderly mule behind him. Pickett tried to stop, but she wasn't fast enough. She slammed into the mule's flanks then crashed to the ground. The cobblestones knocked the back of her head, and for a moment she saw stars. The man yelped. The mule brayed. And there was Spidernose on top of her, gripping the front of her shirt.

"Caught you," he growled.

Pickett groaned, focusing on his face. "Technically the animal did that."

He released the front of her shirt and started patting her all over. "Where is it?"

"Your balls? They're in Lady Elowey's powder jar."

He made it down to her waist, his motions growing more frantic. "The comb! That thing is worth more than a house. Where are you hiding it?"

"I don't know what you're talking about," Pickett said, clicking her fingers together. It would take a few goes, but she could manage it at this close proximity. "Search all you like. You won't find anything."

He got to the pockets at her hips, which held nothing more than a few coins. "If you don't have it, then why did you run?"

"Because I didn't want the spider on your nose to bite me."

She clicked her fingers together again, getting a good, strong spark this time. With a wicked grin, Pickett kicked Spidernose off, just in time for him to catch the smoke drifting up, a small flame spreading across his sleeve. He screamed, rolling around on the street as the other servants removed their vests and started slapping him with them. Pickett would have loved to enjoy the spectacle. If she stuck around much longer, however, they were really going to have a problem with her.

She darted down a side street, winding around a few times before circling back to the temple, just in time for the midday prayer bell to ring through the air. A group of Sedrians, all in wide-brimmed hats or hoods or veils, slipped inside. Pickett hesitated, glancing back toward the Fair Fishman, but Edie wasn't there. Maybe she was still inside, and there were worse places to take cover than this.

Pickett raced to the front of the line, past the fishmongers and washer women and a patroness with a bucket, and into the temple of Al-Dagos.

CHAPTER

TWELVE

Pickett stumbled into a hall suddenly dark as night, right until something cool and solid smashed into her face. Fuck! Did the dragon god have a problem with lanterns, or was running into walls a secret path to wisdom?

Pickett pulled back, rubbing her nose. Even when her eyes started to adjust, it was still hard as hell to see anything. She took a few tentative steps forward, feeling along the wall. Maybe she could find Edie in here and show her the back door. Technically, she was on the job.

Footsteps began to echo through the dark corridor. Without quite knowing what she needed to do, she picked a direction and started walking away from the group with her chin held high. She just had to pretend she belonged there. She definitely belonged there. Nobody ever belonged somewhere as much as she belonged there. And maybe if she belonged here, she could find a good place to hide out, or even where Edie or the Nancy girl were.

"Excuse me" came a sharp voice. "You don't belong here."

Pickett skidded to a stop and turned to see a tall woman with a dragon scale pauldron, her thin face pinched.

Khanah's sunny fucking farts! Pickett pasted on a wide smile and rubbed her hands together.

"Excellent. Just who I was looking for."

The woman arched a brow. "You were looking for me?"

"Well, someone. I seem to have gotten lost. Not sure where I'm meant to show my respects to the great dragon."

The woman narrowed her eyes, but gestured curtly for Pickett to follow her back down the hall, muttering under her breath. "Told them we should put up signs."

They stopped just outside a pair of ornate doors where a large wicker box sat conspicuously close to the path of traffic. The woman pulled out a sheer cloth, then, looking Pickett over, selected a larger one.

"Keep your whole head covered while you pray," she reminded her. "Some fool came in earlier wearing a skirt as a veil. It would have been embarrassing even without her hair sticking out like the middle of a daisy."

Pickett had to fight to keep her queasy smile as she accepted the veil. Had Edie been kicked out? Was she looking for her? No need to panic. Edie could be flexible, as could Pickett.

"Some people really don't understand tradition. I hope she didn't offend him."

The woman blinked once, then twice. "Who?"

"Al-Dagos. Big dragon god."

The woman looked like Pickett had just jammed a handful of sour bibblewood berries down her throat.

"*She*," the woman corrected tartly, "dwells in the waters, not in the temple. We veil ourselves to cut off outside influence so we can focus only on receiving her wisdom."

Pickett's cheeks burned. "Right. Well if she's not here, then how do you—"

The woman gestured sharply at the doors. "You may pay your respects, and leave me to my duties. Thank you."

Clearly, Al-Dagos was not the patron deity of congeniality.

Pickett sniffed and draped the veil over her head. It only just managed to cover her hair with an inch or two overlap, and immediately it cut off all view of the world. She wondered idly how many devotees smacked into walls or tripped over chairs while coming in for their sacred prayers.

She dared to raise the bottom of her veil, just to avoid tripping over any of the other people kneeling on the floor in front of what appeared to be an impressive indoor fountain. Light filtered in from above them, making the water glitter like crystal in the otherwise dark room. The other worshippers sat on the ground, legs crossed and hands resting palm-up on their knees. It would have been very moving if Pickett hadn't just learned they actually knew exactly where the dragon was and it wasn't here. Weakly, she glanced around in case Edie was still here, but no. She was alone, but maybe one of the people in here was Nancy.

Pickett sank down, mimicking the others as she let her eyes adjust to the poor light. The veil wasn't completely opaque. After a couple of minutes, she could just start to make out shapes and colors. That was something, at least. Now she could probably make it out of the room once she actually knew the next step.

She leaned over to the person next to her and whispered, "I can't see a thing. Are we in the guest section or the patroness section? Are the new ones mixed in or do they keep them strictly in groups?"

The person turned to her, held up a finger to the front of their veil, and let out a sharp *ssh!*

That probably wasn't her. Pickett shuffled to another section, searching out someone who looked like they lived here while being young enough to be her girl. There was a small gaggle of girls all hunched together in the back. Pickett sat next to them and tried to make out their shapes. Damn. She should have asked what Nancy looked like.

A new figure sat down next to her and Pickett stiffened, trying her best to look like a dutiful worshipper.

"New here?"

"Um."

"You're wearing a temple veil," the strange woman whispered. "Most people at least come in with their own. Better than the lady with the skirt."

"Surprised you could see her under these things." Pickett tugged at the edge of her own veil, loosing a couple of curls on the other side.

The woman snorted. "I didn't have to. Everyone was talking about her earlier. She came too early, though. I assume that's why you're here?"

Pickett frowned and leaned in closer. "Nancy?"

The woman stiffened. "No...I'm Rhee. Are you not Shay?"

Pickett heaved a sigh. Maybe it was for the best that she didn't make contact. Once this service wrapped up, hopefully Elowey's men would be gone so she could safely return to the room.

An old woman shuffled up onto the stage and started muttering something about wisdom and understanding. Pickett was more interested in the exits. She probably shouldn't leave through the same door she came in. If she followed the patronesses out, she might be able to dodge anyone on the street waiting for her to leave through the main entrance.

When the old woman stopped talking, everyone made a complicated gesture with their hands. Pickett idly wiggled her wrists before rising, following Rhee and the other patronesses out, opposite to the direction of the other congregants. At least until they took a right through the dark corridors, and Pickett took a left.

She smacked right into a closed door.

"Fucking titmashers," she hissed, rubbing her nose. For

people who worshipped a wisdom-dragon, they sure liked to stay in the dark.

She turned and nearly barreled into a patroness standing right in the middle of the hallway.

"Um…" Pickett cleared her throat. "Sorry. I got lost. I'll see myself out."

"Are you looking for someone?" the patroness whispered.

Pickett blinked. "It depends on if there's a certain someone here who wants to be found."

"I knew it!" She grabbed Pickett's wrist and yanked her down the darkened hall. "I knew my sweet man would send someone for me. My father can get stuffed."

Nancy! Pickett grinned and picked up her pace to keep up.

Nancy shoved through another door, and for a moment Pickett was blinded again, this time by the open sunlight beating down on her. Nancy tugged Pickett next to the fountain before ripping off her veil. Pickett did the same and blinked, taking in the wide courtyard filled with leafy shrubs and half-wild garden patches. At its center was another fountain, this one larger and louder with a sculpted dragon jutting out of the middle, belching out water like it had eaten too much. For a cloister, it was pretty luxurious, and Nancy looked like she belonged.

She had a full face and dark, perfect curlspinned up into an elegant bun. Everything about her spoke of someone who'd never had to go hungry in her life. And yet she had that look about her of someone always on the edge of a frown. Perhaps the wealthy were not always happy. But there was something else about her. Something familiar.

Nancy held a finger to her lips as she dropped a stone into the fountain behind them. The *plop* was barely audible under the fountain, but a sudden buzz filled the air as dozens of tiny brown bugs launched up from the water. For a moment, Pickett was prepared to swat at what looked like bitterbugs before they could hitch a ride home with her and decimate the food stores of the Pick's Pocket. But how could they be bitterbugs in the humid climate? A closer inspection showed their yellowed fingernail abdomens with wings four times the size of their bodies.

"We call them buzzles," Nancy explained. "Some sort of mutant. We think a few rode in with some traders and their babies adapted to the climate. As far as we can tell, they've never reproduced outside of the temple, never even left the waters here as far as we can tell. They like to stick close to home. The patronesses sometimes use them in rituals. Cutting out sound to make it easier to focus on Al-Dagos."

"And to make it harder to hear a private conversation from a distance." Pickett held out a finger. The buzzle poked at it with its spiny snout, then went back to buzzing around in the air.

"We only have a few minutes until they settle back down." Nancy gripped Pickett's hand. "But I was right, wasn't I? You were sent to retrieve me?"

"Yeah. Though I have to say, I feel a lot better about committing holy treason if you don't want to be here."

Nancy scoffed. "My father didn't approve of my suitor. He thought keeping me here until he found a more acceptable one would be the end of that. I'm afraid I'll simply never be able to forgive him, but it's fine. I told him my future husband would make good on his promise to find help and break me out."

Well this was going swimmingly. Nancy's lover had to be loaded and desperate if he was willing to pay up to two suns to cross a dragon god and free her. He must have also been a dunderhead to hire Simon, but here they all were.

Pickett rose and tugged Nancy's hand. "Right. If that's how you feel, come with me. I've got a place to stash you until we can finish the job."

But Nancy didn't rise. And there it was. The frown that had been dancing on the edge of her expression earlier.

"I'm afraid it's not so simple," she confessed, releasing Pickett's hand so she could tug one of her sleeves up. There on her forearm looked to be some sort of tattoo in a strange configuration of sharp angles and looping curves. Pickett had no idea what it meant, but it was easy enough to guess what it was.

"Runes?"

Nancy nodded and tugged her sleeve back down.

"My father also hired a runecrafter to keep me here. This keeps me from leaving the temple."

Right. Well that complicated things. And already, the buzzles were calming down. Pickett chewed the inside of her cheek and nodded to herself. "Good news is I don't think someone has to be a sorcerer to use runes. And better news is I know someone who uses them."

Nancy's bright eyes widened and she clasped her fingers together. "Really? That's wonderful. When can you bring them in?"

"As soon as we figure out how she can break the hold on you." Pickett winked. "Don't you worry. We'll bust you out before—"

"Nancy" came a melodic voice, followed by the even click of heels on stone. Nancy jumped to her feet, blood draining from her face. They both turned to see a woman dressed in a gown the color of dried blood, a boiled leather cuirass over her chest. Markings like the runes Pickett had seen in Edie's pamphlet laced up her fingers. As she flexed her hands, they shifted and resettled like sand disturbed.

Nancy balled her hands into fists. "This is just a friend of mine. She came to visit. That's all."

"A friend?" The woman stepped forward, scowling as she planted her hands on her hips. "Or a fox come to spring a little bird from its cage?"

"I'm not one of my father's pets, Corsa!"

Wait. Pets? Who did Pickett know who kept birds as pets?

Who also had dark, curly hair and a full, plump, attractive face and figure?

"Your name wouldn't happen to be Nancy Fistic, would it?"

Corsa smirked. "Some friend just learning your name, Nancy. I suppose your father didn't buy her for you, did he?"

Pickett stared at the woman, then at Nancy, then raised her gaze to the sky above.

"*Fuck!*"

THIRTEEN

Nancy, are you really sure you want to leave? This seems like a nice temple," Pickett said, waving her hand through the air and smacking a few buzzles in the process. They buzzed all the louder and jabbed at her finger, though it hurt about as much as the tip of a trimmed nail.

Nancy turned on her, eyes wide. "You're supposed to be helping me," she hissed.

"Yes, well, maybe I'm helping you to not cross your father, whoever that is."

Nancy's jaw fell open for a moment. A buzzle flew right in. She sputtered, spitting it onto the ground.

"Excuse me," Corsa cut in. Her arms were crossed, her expression pinched as she glanced between the two of them. "Are you going to leave or am I going to have to make you leave?"

"She's not going anywhere!" Nancy snapped, grabbing Pickett's elbow.

Pickett jerked back. "Hang on, don't speak for me."

"Are you scared of my father?"

"I'm scared of what he'll do if he finds out I tried to break you out." Pickett planted her hands on her hips. Fuck. Who did Nancy fall in love with? The Gilt King? No. If that was the case, then Fistic would have uncovered his identity.

"I'm going to take this as both of you choosing to make me work." Corsa sighed, raising her hand.

Nancy's eyes widened and she shouted, "Corsa, don't—"

But before she could finish, Corsa made some complex moves with her hands. Pickett's gut churned as she was pretty sure those complex moves involved Corsa's hands bending backward. With a screech, she flung her arms forward.

There was a soft ripple in the air. The world slowed as the smell of lightning flooded the courtyard. Then the buzzles shot up as fire burst forth from Corsa's palms, slithering through the air like an eel headed for Pickett and only Pickett.

Pickett didn't have time to think, not consciously anyway. Her subconscious screamed a lot of things like *"Shit fuck damn ass cunt"* as her body moved, throwing up the edge of her cloak as though she could somehow hide from a magical fire monster. Her conscious mind though? That was as empty as a keg after the sailors came through.

The world grew hot. Then less hot. Then cool. Pickett blinked. Through the fabric, Edie's careful stitches glowed like stars. She thought back to the way Edie made the chalk rune move back in the Fair Fishman and grinned.

A single thought entered her mind. *You can't touch me, bitch.*

She flung back the cape to see a very startled-looking Corsa and Nancy, and as much as Pickett wanted to gloat, she had the feeling that, sooner or later, the sorceress would find a way to touch her.

Clearly, Nancy had the same thought because she grabbed Pickett's wrist and shouted, "Come on!"

Pickett swore but didn't resist as Nancy raced to the other side of the courtyard, knocking stray buzzles out of the air as she charged right back into the hallway.

Wham!

Sparks burst before her eyes as pain bloomed out from the center of her face. Right. These halls were pretty narrow and it was dark. But Pickett was pretty sure she hadn't broken her nose.

"Don't stop," Nancy gasped.

Suddenly Pickett found herself being dragged down the hall, running well before her eyes had time to adjust. "Where are we going?"

"Back door. You can sneak out," Nancy explained. "Go through the rum joint next door. Their kitchen shares a wall with a stable. Hide there with some of the horses. Corsa won't work that hard to find you, trust me."

"You mean us?"

"I can't leave, remember. She won't hurt me," Nancy insisted. "My father hired her to keep an eye on me."

Rock scraped against rock as the floor trembled beneath them. Pickett stumbled forward, grasping Nancy's shoulders to keep her balance.

"Oh she's really pissed," Nancy squeaked. She grabbed Pickett's arm and raced around the corner. They passed patronesses shouting or yelping in dismay.

"Why did we ever let a runecrafter into these hallowed halls?" one cried while another gesticulated angrily. Pickett assumed she'd taken a vow of silence, and this was her way of agreeing.

It wasn't a big temple, and soon enough Nancy led Pickett to an unobtrusive wooden door. She kicked it open and pointed at a ramshackle mud brick building a few meters away.

"It'll only work as a hiding spot once, so go," Nancy insisted. "Don't stay too long. Sing *Lady Lad* in your head three times then leave before she comes looking for you."

"Okay, fine, but aren't you interested in leaving with me?"

"I . . ." Nancy caught her breath, glanced over her shoulder, then turned back, her eyes shining in the dim light. "Just get somewhere safe."

Nancy shoved Pickett through the door. Pickett staggered onto the half-cobbled side street, kicking up sand as Nancy cried out.

Pickett turned, blinking against the bright sun. Nancy hunched just close enough to the exit that she was awash in light, but her feet remained firmly planted inside the temple. She clutched her forearm, and blood dripped out from her sleeve. Tears streamed down her cheeks as she tugged the bloody sleeve up over the rune. It looked like it had been freshly slashed into her skin. Under the blood, the symbol itself shone like lightning.

So that's what happened if she tried to leave. Pickett's blood curdled at the sight and she wanted to scream or puke or some combination of the two. Sure, she was a rich girl being looked after in a relatively cozy temple. But Nancy was as much a prisoner as Pickett had been during her servitude. Moreso, in fact. And it was Nancy's own father who was responsible.

Nancy staggered back away from the light. The blood stopped flowing from her arm, the skin knitting itself back together neatly.

Pickett balled her hands into fists. Suddenly, it didn't matter that every patroness in the temple might bring a dragon's wrath onto her. It didn't matter that Fistic could fuck her and the bar six times over or that Corsa could cook her like a leg of lamb. She'd fight the sun itself to get Nancy out of there.

"I promise. I'll figure out how to get rid of that rune."

Nancy nodded, her eyes still red with tears.

"Go," she hissed. "You can't help me if Corsa catches you."

And with that, Nancy ducked back into the temple, shutting the door behind her.

FOURTEEN

Pickett stumbled into the rum bar, shoving past patrons and workers alike. In the kitchens, a maid took one look at her and rolled her eyes.

"Let me guess. Another patroness is smuggling out a lover?" she scoffed.

Pickett didn't bother to respond to that. She shoved through the door, right into the familiar barn smell. None of the horses looked safe to hide with, but one of the stalls had a few goats. She hopped over it and ducked behind a mound of straw. The goats bleated and one shot out a few pellets of dung, but otherwise caused no commotion.

Pickett would have heaved a sigh of relief if her heart wasn't racing like a dragonfly's wings. Just the thought of that mark on Nancy's arm made her blood curdle. It was one thing for Fistic to hide her away and hire a sorceress to keep her there. But that mark. What kind of twisted heart could do that to his own child? She tried to rectify that with the man who fed his birds during their meetings. The man who honored her debt when it was paid off. He was a greedy man, a selfish and shrewd man, but he'd never struck her as cruel.

A goat wandered up to her and, after a sniff, began to nibble on the corner of her cape. Her very protective, very powerful cape. Pickett shoved its snout aside and began reciting in her head the song Nancy had mentioned.

> Lady Lad, oh Lady Lad
> She was the best I ever had.
> With rosy cheeks and fire hair
> My lady lad, she got me there.
> And as affection grew and grew,
> She said, "I'm feeling something new."
> Now breeches over skirts, today
> And thus the lad came out to play.
> He may switch back or he may not,
> A changing treasure's what I've got.
> Oh Lady Lad, oh Lady Lad
> He was the best I ever had.

It was a favorite in the brothels of Southfen, and Pickett had learned it within a week of living in the Spotted Dick.

When she finished the verse for the third time, Pickett dared to slip out the front. It didn't look like any fire-friendly runecrafters were stalking the streets. Still, she tried to lay low as she scurried back to the Fair Fishman. Edie sat on the stoop out front, worrying the bottom of her skirt so violently she might have worn a hole into the fabric with her thumb. At Pickett's approach, she leaped from her spot and threw herself forward, wrapping her arms tightly around Pickett's shoulders.

"Where were you?" she cried as she pulled back. "The temple kicked me out before the prayer service even started because of my headwear, so I thought we could regroup and you were just gone and—"

"Yeah. It's complicated," Pickett said, squeezing Edie's hands. "Let's get to the room, and I'll tell you everything."

Edie nodded, and they headed inside. On the way to the stairs, a man reached out a hand. "My lady witch—"

"Fresh out of lucky charms, I'm afraid," she said before taking the steps two at a time. Only once they were in the stairwell did Pickett dare to start whispering. "I found Nancy, but there are runes on her. They draw blood if she tries to leave. And she's Fistic's daughter."

"What?" Edie hissed, her eyes going wide. "Pickett, this is bad. We don't need to cross him."

"No, we do not," Pickett agreed, digging through her pockets for the room key. "Not to mention . . ."

She froze. The doorframe was splintered near the knob, and the door itself was cracked. Not much. Not enough to see into the room. But just enough to notice.

"Pickett—"

Pickett held up her hand and gestured to the door. Edie clenched her jaw, eyes wide. She gave a little nod and took a step back. Pickett pressed her ear to the wood, trying not to think about what part of the naked painted fishman she leaned against. There was no creak of floorboards, no rustling of anything. She bit the inside of her cheek, then gave a nod before pushing the door open.

There was nobody there, but there had been. The bedding had been tossed about the room. Their overnight bags lay open, their contents strewn around like guts.

"What happened?" Edie breathed, but Pickett doubted it was because she didn't know. No doubt, she just needed something to say.

"My guess is someone rented a room so they'd be allowed upstairs," Pickett said grimly, crouching next to her bag and rifling through the damage. "They probably figured out which room was ours and busted in."

Fuck. Pickett ran her fingers over the bits of broken glass under her spare clothes. Two of her blackout bottles had survived, but the rest of her "witch" supplies were just gone. No more colored flames. No tricks if she really needed them. Either the looters had known or they had just wanted to spite her by destroying something random.

"Was this Fistic?" Edie gasped. Already, she was stuffing her things back into her overnight bag.

Pickett wanted to insist it couldn't be. This wasn't Fistic's style. He had too much class. But she remembered the mark on Nancy's arm. Anyone who'd do that to his own daughter had no class at all.

"I won't speak to his credit, but this isn't his style," Pickett said, glancing around the room. "He tends to approach people directly. He gives them a chance to back down. But he's not the only rich dick I've got to deal with."

Edie paused halfway through stuffing the skirt she'd worn into the temple back into her bag. And that's when Pickett noticed it. The day bag she wore draped over her shoulder. That was it, wasn't it? Fuck, she really had been drunk, hadn't she?

"Pickett?"

Pickett heaved a sigh and held out her hand. "Edie, can I have your bag?"

"What?"

"I made another mistake. And it'll be easiest to show you."

Edie furrowed her brows as she slipped the bag off, holding it out. "What did you do?"

"Fucked up. What else is new?" Pickett rifled through the bag and, sure enough, there it was. She sank down onto the bed, holding up the comb with its fine pearl inlays. The comb that would have looked so lovely in Edie's hair. "I think our room was trashed by some people looking for this. The thing is, Lady Elowey was an ass, and I worked in her house for a little while. She never seemed to pay much attention to this thing, and I thought it'd be nice to bring you back something pretty. To say sorry for all the trouble."

Edie stared at her for a long moment, then blinked slowly and shook her head. "Trouble?"

"I mean"—Pickett gestured vaguely with the comb—"I didn't tell you about the debt I owed Fistic, and that got us into trouble. Then I had to ditch you for months and you're the one who got me out early, which isn't fair to you. But Lady Elowey's men chased me down on the street. When they couldn't find it on my person, they must have figured I'd stashed it in our room."

Edie just kept shaking her head until she coughed. Which turned out to be a sort of laugh. Then she laughed more and sank down onto the bed, resting her hand on Pickett's wrist.

"You mean all this is because you wanted to bring me a present?"

Pickett shrugged. "Yes?"

"Pickett." Edie squeezed her wrist before letting go, folding her hands in her lap. "I don't need that. I've told you a hundred times. You gave me a home. I've never had that before."

"You mean a home that's falling apart in the middle of a swamp," Pickett scoffed.

Edie nudged her shoulder. "It's better now. We've got well-behaved patrons. I've got an investor who doesn't charge interest from right out of our asses."

"An investor I haven't met in person."

"And yet you didn't complain." Edie sighed and wrapped an arm around Pickett's shoulder. "I've met him. I like him. Isn't that enough?"

"I like you, that doesn't mean I like everybody you like."

"That's because you hardly like anybody." Edie shrugged and smiled. "Well, back to the point, at least. You know I adore you. I really do. Which is exactly why I don't need fancy gifts."

"You deserve them."

"I don't need them," Edie replied firmly. "I have you and Letterboy and Hoag and the bar. I have all I need. So you keep that on you. If they show up again, say you magically procured it for them."

Something warm bloomed in Pickett's chest, but she rolled her eyes. "And you think they'll believe that?"

Edie laughed and plucked something from Pickett's curls. She held it up, revealing a dead buzzle between her fingers. Pickett's cheeks burned.

"Rich people like riches," Edie said, flicking the bug aside. "They get those riches and we get our adventures. Though I admit it makes the room less comfortable."

"I suppose so," Picket grumbled, glancing around. Even if they locked the room, the Eloweys had already busted through it once. They'd do it again.

She flopped back onto the bed.

"I've got one place I think we can go," she admitted. "But it's a little tawdry."

Edie flopped onto the bed next to her. "We killed a man and run a bounty hunter bar. Leave a note for your brother and let's get going. Nothing left can scandalize me."

FIFTEEN

The sun had already set, but the Spotted Dick somehow shone like a beacon, with lanterns hanging all over it, light bouncing off the white paint. Maybe that was why the Gilt King had decided to paint it that color. Fistic had mentioned some of the Gilt King's properties had been renovated. When they went inside, would she even recognize it?

The doors to the balcony remained shut, but Pickett could just imagine the office beyond them, and all the warm days and breezy nights she'd spent up there.

Pickett grabbed Edie's hand and gave it a squeeze, her eyes fixed on that balcony.

"Remind me what you did when you worked here," Edie said, eyeing the building suspiciously.

Pickett rolled her eyes. "It's not what you think. I was an accountant and it was a long time go."

Edie squeezed the strap of her pack. "It looks very busy."

And that was true. There was a line, an actual line, of sailors out the door. How good must a place be to make a man willing to wait possibly hours for a room in a brothel? Especially since the Spotted Dick was hardly the only establishment of its kind on the street.

Pickett took a sharp breath and shrugged. "Maybe busy will be good. We can melt into the crowd. Besides, if the Gilt King owns this place, Fistic won't fuck with it. Not now anyway. So even if he does find out it was me in the temple—"

Edie frowned deeply. "So we trust in the protection of a perfect stranger?"

"Not exactly."

Pickett grabbed Edie's hand and shoved her way past customers, earning a few nasty remarks in the process. Inside, the place was packed, with hardly any of the dames outside of their rooms to flirt with potential customers. Only a couple of harried young ladies darted back and forth with wine. One paused, looking ready to faint as she stared at them with wide eyes.

"Lady or fella?" she asked. "Because if you're here for the fella, he's presently engaged and someone's in line so it'll be a wait, but it'll be faster if you're here for a lady, especially if you're here together so—"

"No, no, no," Edie squeaked.

The girl heaved a world-weary sigh and shifted from one foot to another. "Well, we ain't hiring. We're busting at the seams taking in all those girls from Gristlark. You should go try the Pirate's Puss."

Edie managed to look even more scandalized at that idea. Pickett squeezed her hand and stared hard at the girl.

"Don't worry. We're just here to talk to Merca."

That didn't seem to make the girl feel any better, but she didn't seem more likely to keel over as she scurried off.

Edie slunk back against the wall, staring around the place with wide eyes. "You used to live here?"

"Come on. It's not so different from the Pick's Pocket," Pickett insisted. "I mean, it's a place of joy. Of booze."

Edie wrinkled her nose as a ruddy-faced man stumbled down the stairs, grinning from ear to ear and stinking of a very particular act. He blinked at them, then staggered against the wall, his grin widening.

"You're new," he hummed, reaching for Pickett, but his hand landed on Edie's shoulder. "I just got paid and I can afford a little more though I'll need an hour or so."

Edie stiffened like the first frost. Pickett leaned over to swat his hand away.

"Save your coin for the Dick Dames, sailor," she said. "We're in other business."

"And what sort is that?" he purred, leering at them both.

That was enough of that. Pickett shook her hand, flicking her flints together. She didn't have any colored powders or special tricks, but the quick spark from her fingers had the man stumbling back, muttering "demon" as he staggered outside, his breeches not even fully laced.

Edie sagged against Pickett. "Not to insult the place, but I hate it."

Pickett patted her shoulder. "I promise, it isn't always like this." Or, at least, it wasn't always like this. What happened to the time when the dames had to hang out the windows to advertise their services? Was this the work of the Gilt King? Most importantly, was this better or worse than it had been before?

She just had to hope they were safe here.

Someone tutted to her right, and Pickett glanced over to see Merca standing there, draped in yellow silks. She didn't have the pipe this time, but something about her remained perfectly, flawlessly elegant. The signs of age on her face only granted her an additional layer of wisdom. Pickett was willing to believe she was a goddess before any sort of distant dragon.

"Pickett," she purred, stepping forward to look her up and down. "What have you done?"

Pickett's face burned. Edie glanced between her and Merca before she stepped forward.

"We just need a place to hide out for a little while."

"Yes, yes." Merca flicked her wrist at Edie before cupping Pickett's chin. "Darling, I see your pores. And I don't think I can spot a single hair that hasn't been split."

A lump formed in her throat. Pickett swallowed it down and forced a smile. "Where I'm working, now, that's not really my priority."

"It ought to be." Merca cocked her head to the side with a smirk. "You're still the loveliest office girl I ever had."

Her eyes stung. How could this hurt and feel good at the same time? Why had Pickett left Merca? Why had she decided to flee from the only person who ever gave her a lasting home?

"Loveliest? I thought I was the hardest working."

"If you took fewer smoke breaks." Merca laughed. "And don't go with most educated, because I had to teach you half the numbers myself."

Fuck. She had, hadn't she? If Pickett had remembered more of Merca's lessons, she might have done better with the bar, avoided indenture, avoided the years apart.

Edie stepped forward, holding out her free hand. "I'm Edaneth. I go by Edie. I work with Pickett in our bar, mostly in the kitchens."

"A bar?" Merca laughed. "But you hardly drink at all."

Edie let out a sharp laugh, but Merca shot her a befuddled look.

"Wait." Edie frowned, glancing between them. "This one didn't drink?"

"Has that changed?" Merca asked.

Pickett cleared her throat. "Yes, um, I keep busy." She held up a hand. "Keeping the spirit of this place alive through other ventures but . . . We agreed to do a job here for some extra coin. And it took a turn."

"Mm." Merca nodded, glancing between them before she shrugged. "You're a dame, Pickett. And nobody's sleeping in the office. I've been doing the books for a good while , and I have my own room."

Pickett could have sagged. But she didn't. She had just enough pride to stand straight and nod. "Thank you, Merca. We really appreciate it."

"Of course." Merca squeezed her shoulder. "I'll send a girl with food. Edie can settle in the office while you and I beautify."

"That isn't necessary."

"It isn't negotiable."

MERCA'S ROOM was different than Pickett remembered it. A bit more cluttered and cozy. She clearly didn't take customers anymore, which made the place all the more hers. Merca gripped Pickett's shoulder firmly as she steered her to a wide vanity and began tutting over her hair.

"Now I see why you never let it grow this long back in the day. You could use a trim at some point. If you like, I could get one of the girls to trim it back as short as it used to be. Give you less to deal with."

Pickett stiffened. Back in the day, it was just short enough to gather into a small, tight bun, small enough to fit in his... Her heart skipped a beat. She'd buried that man beneath the time she'd spent running her bar. The time before that begging for rides and taking odd jobs to pay to get back home. All the years between the present and the last time she felt she deserved to be in this brothel had smothered his name. Yet, here it was, summoned by the place where she'd first met him.

Patr.

Patr Patr Patr.

Her love. The prick.

"No," she murmured. By all the gods living and dead, she didn't want any part of her to be small enough to fit in someone's hand, not ever again.

Merca frowned, but said nothing as she opened a jar, palming a little oil that smelled like flowers and fresh cut wood. Pickett closed her eyes and breathed it in. Merca always had access to such fine things, the newest scents, the softest sheets. Perhaps if she'd stayed, Pickett could have learned to be like Merca. But that door closed behind her when she left.

It was only as Merca was deep in the work of twisting her hair into something lovelier than Pickett could manage alone that she started up again.

"So your friend seems lovely, but I rather expected you to arrive here with someone else. What became of your young man?"

Ah, of course this was going to come up. Pickett balled her hands into fists and swallowed thickly, keeping her eyes firmly shut.

"Gone."

"Gone? As in split or dead?"

"I-I don't know," Pickett admitted. "But if it isn't one, it's certainly the other."

Merca's hands stilled. "Oh darling."

"It's fine," Pickett insisted, opening her eyes so she could have something to focus on. She stared hard at a broken bracelet, analyzing every bead that sat alone on the table. No, it wasn't alone but surrounded by other beads. "I run a bar in the Rottering swamp, now. With Edie. Got regular performers. I have a dancing, singing sailor who brings in crowds. It's not too unlike what Kaz did back in the day. Remember Kaz?"

"The swamp, though?" Merca demanded, her hands falling to Pickett's shoulders. "That's not a kind place. I don't doubt you put on a show, but you chose quite a place to do it."

"I've got ways to keep safe." Pickett snapped and couldn't

help smiling as Merca jumped back at the sparks that flew from her fingers.

"Goodness," Merca breathed. "You always were a clever one, weren't you?"

"Had to be." Pickett shrugged. "It wasn't . . . I mean, after Patr and I split, things got hard. I had to find anything I could to hold on to."

"You could have come back here."

Pickett shook her head, her stomach twisting. "Not after how I left."

"I'd have smoothed it over for you," Merca insisted, but it was empty words and they both knew it.

"It's fine, really," Pickett murmured. "I have a home. I have Edie. I wanted to let the past stay where it was."

"Yes, well, would that it were so." Merca gave Pickett's shoulder a rub before she swept away, digging through some of the clutter that had accumulated next to her nightstand. Pickett turned, careful not to move too quickly and ruin her half-finished hair. After a moment, Merca rose, holding what appeared to be a letter.

"This arrived a few years ago," she explained, handing it to Pickett.

The letter was bound with an unfamiliar seal, just circles within circles. But on the front, in an all-too-familiar scrawl, were words she didn't care to read.

To Pickett

From Patr

"Perhaps he thought you'd come back home," Merca explained gently.

So he saw this as Pickett's home. He didn't see it the way she had. That, by running with him, she'd turned her back on Merca and the dames the way Simon had turned his back on her.

She ran her thumb over the wax seal, careful not to break it. The was old and cheap. If she wasn't careful, she might accidentally have to read what he said.

"Good to know he's still alive," she mused. "Or at least he was when we parted."

Merca watched her for a long moment, hands folded together before she nodded. "I don't suppose you care to open it?"

"Not really." Pickett tucked the letter in the pocket of her cape and sniffed. No tears. Not now. Not ever. "Edie and I aren't just here to stay the night. I think we've stumbled into some trouble."

Merca's lip quirked. "Why am I not surprised?"

"Maybe because you could be caught in it too." Pickett cleared her throat and sat up a little straighter. "We were hired for a job. A job which may have us crossing Southfen's favorite moneylender."

"Fistic." Merca rolled her eyes. "That man will never be content."

"I suspect neither will the current owner of the Spotted Dick." Pickett rose and crossed her arms. "Word on the street is a new greedy bastard's trying to compete with the old greedy bastard, and said greedy bastard is the reason for the fresh coat of paint outside."

"Ah." Merca didn't look surprised, just resigned. "The Gilt King. Dreadful name, but once people assign it, I imagine even the richest man on the continent couldn't snuff it out."

"Quite the guy," Pickett said dryly, glancing around the room. "And you're all right with a complete stranger owning all of this?"

"Not all right, but we would have gone under without him," Merca said, shaking her head. "I want to hope he'll pass on like all the other owners, but who knows when that will be?"

"Maybe you can convince him to sell," Pickett said. In a sudden burst of affection, like a rabbit leaping from a box, she grabbed Merca's hand and gave it a squeeze. "Fistic and the Gilt King may be going to war. And Fistic has a runecrafter on his side. Every single establishment they own will be at risk."

Merca grimaced, but nodded. "I respect that. I do, darling. But I can't negotiate with a man I can't meet, and I don't have the money to buy this place off of him."

"Then leave when it gets dangerous," Pickett insisted. "You can come to the swamp. The Pick's Pocket isn't special, but it's safe. Edie's a pretty good cook. We've got shelter and beer and rum, if you need."

"Oh, Pickett." Merca sighed as she cupped Pickett's cheek. "My job is to keep this place running. I see to the kitchens. I manage the girls and the clients. I keep them safe. Unless you could convince each one of them to leave, I'm afraid we'll be staying here."

"But Merca—"

"None of that." She tutted and caught Pickett's chin. "Now sit. I'm only half done with your hair. If I'm going to be sending you back to that bar when you're done here, I can at least send you in style."

CHAPTER

SIXTEEN

I t had been a long time since Pickett had been dressed like this. Even in the Elowey estate, she was given the shabbiest uniform as a new and only temporary servant, but Merca did nothing by halves. After the incident in the temple, Pickett insisted on keeping her cape. Merca, however, was nothing if not persistent. So Pickett had been forced to swap out her practical trousers for a skirt with little golden leaves embroidered along the hem, just the shade to match the charms Merca had braided in, right before the back of Pickett's hair burst free like the frothy tops of water grass. It felt like she was a walking target, begging to be robbed. But she was among the dames. Here, when people saw the gold and the silk, they *gave* money just to win a little time with them.

Pickett felt like someone else. She felt like Merca.

In the main room where eager customers held glasses of colorful drinks, either sipping or sharing stories of their time with one of the dames, Edie sat at the edge of the bar, worrying one of the fraying patches on her bodice. At Pickett's approach, she jumped to her feet, then stumbled back, eyes wide.

"Pickett. You look . . ."

"Merca insisted." Pickett went to play with some of her hair, but it had been braided back, leaving her face fully visible for the world to see. Had she been growing it out to change her look, or had she been doing it to hide?

Merca wrapped an arm around Pickett's shoulders and squeezed. "Our girl was always able to pull off a little fashion. If only she believed in it."

"It's a waste of money," Pickett insisted, ducking out of Merca's grasp. "Besides, I'm not a dame."

Merca scoffed. "I'm not a dame, anymore, either. Doesn't mean I can't look fabulous in my semi-retirement. Come now, Edie. Won't you tell this girl how lovely she looks?"

Lovely like a stray cat in a crown, and Pickett was ready to say as much.

But the way Edie was looking at her, there was no lie in her voice when she said, "You look nice. Really nice."

"See? I work wonders," Merca declared.

Pickett's cheeks burned. With her blue eyes shining in the flickering lamplight and her yellow hair piled on her head like a crown of dandelions, Edie was the prettiest thing Pickett ever knew. But now she was returning the compliment. For one mad moment, Pickett wanted to do this. Do her hair and wash her face apply color to her eyes. She wanted to look pretty for Edie.

The sudden realization of exactly what that meant killed the notion before it could grow into a proper thought. No. Not this place. Not this night. She couldn't let herself think those thoughts in the same building where she'd given her heart away once before.

She needed Edie to stop looking at her the way Patr used to.

Pickett cleared her throat. "Right. Do you still have your pamphlet? I got a good look at Nancy's runes, so maybe we can figure out what to do about it."

The tension snapped like a taut line, and Pickett all but breathed a sigh of relief as Edie nodded, suddenly determined as she turned back to the bar. Shepulled the pamphlet out of her pocket, spreading it out on the counter. Pickett settled on a stool to her right, Merca to her left.

Edie tapped the inked runes. "It looks like the first three are for protection."

Pickett ran her fingers over some of the embroidery on the border of her cape. "Yeah. We can confirm those work. But they're not the ones on Nancy."

Edie shrugged. "That makes sense. I can't seem to get the others to stick in my head right. Whoever would want to do something like this to our girl probably can't manage to protect anything." She tapped the paper. "So this one is to prevent food poisoning. This one is to"—she shook her head, clearing her throat—"I mean, yeah, for masculine, um, difficulties."

"Don't need runes to deal with that," Merca scoffed. "You can handle it with some skill or a little creative pivoting. I should introduce whoever wrote this for you to Trillia. She's new, but she's a true savant."

"Anyway," Edie said loudly, dragging her finger down the pictures and scribbles. "Pickett, do any of these look right?"

Edie flipped the pamphlet over, showing off the drawing and brief descriptions there. Pickett squinted.

"There were a lot of them but I remember that one there, with the three lines. And this jagged round one. Except there was another one kind of slashed in the middle."

"Straight across or slanted? Can you draw it?"

Pickett didn't have to focus hard to summon the image, not that she tried. The blood welling up on Nancy's arm was bound to burn itself into her memory forever. "It was slanted, left to right." She gestured with her hand. "I don't want to draw it. Just in case."

Edie's frown deepened. She tapped her fingers on the bar, a wrinkle forming between her brows.

"Well, you look like someone lit a fire in your brain," Merca mused. "Is that good or do you need a drink to cool it off, darling?"

"I think it's not good," Edie murmured. "I don't have that rune in the pamphlet, but I've gotten an idea of how those lines work together. If I'm right, then the one on Nancy isn't just to contain her in the temple. It's to contain her. Plainly. She can't go farther than the caster wants her to go."

The thought made Pickett's gut churn. "That fire-throwing bitch must have put it on her. Nancy started bleeding just trying to leave the building. What happens if she actually disobeys?"

"I can't say for certain, but I'd guess it's not something she should try. Not if she's at all fond of her arm. And unless the caster removes it...I'm afraid there's no good way we can disrupt it without burning or cutting her ourselves."

Merca swore and gestured to the girl behind the bar. In short order, three glasses materialized in front of them. Merca downed hers without hesitation, while Pickett took a healthy swig. It burned on the way down. Clearly, this was not a moment to drink for pleasure.

"This really fucking makes me hate Fistic," Pickett muttered. She'd never liked the guy, but this was just barbaric. Had he really knowingly had that thing put on her? The runecrafter was bad enough. "How do we get Nancy out of there without maiming her?"

Edie chewed on her lip and flipped the pamphlet over again and again. Whatever answer she was looking for, though, must not have been there. She heaved a sigh and, at last, grabbed her own glass, though she didn't drink. Not right away.

"What did you say a moment ago? About the runecrafter?"

"That she was a fire throwing bitch," Pickett answered. "Nearly singed my nose off. I'd come up with something more creative but that's the best I can think to call her at the moment."

"Then she can't be the one who put that rune on Nancy,"

Edie said. "Runecrafters work in specialties. I'm still trying to figure out what mine is, but if she throws fire . . ."

"So, what, we have another mystery magical fuck on the sidelines?" Pickett scoffed.

Edie fiddled with a loose thread on her sleeve. "I need to go back to the bar," she said. "There's something there I need. It may be able to help."

Pickett's chest tightened. "What, are you hiding a secret weapon in the kitchen?"

Edie wrinkled her nose. "Yes and no. It's hard to explain. I need to consult someone, a sort of expert."

"I'll go with you."

"No. You need to stay and make sure Nancy isn't moved elsewhere."

Pickett needed to stay. Edie needed to go. It was all happening again, in this place. She was going to be alone again. Pickett balled one hand into a fist as she knocked back the rest of her drink. The burn down her throat was a decent distraction, even if only a temporary one.

"Hey." Edie squeezed her wrist. "I'll be gone a day at most. I'll be back, I promise."

Simon had left without a word. Patr, well, he'd never made a promise exactly. They were just words, but Pickett managed to clench her jaw, twisting her hand so she could lace her fingers through Edie's.

"Let's talk about it later," Pickett insisted. "Simon and Jodiah will be here in another day. One of them can go with you if I can't. Deal?"

Edie sighed but nodded. "Deal."

CHAPTER

SEVENTEEN

I f anyone asked why Pickett was up late, keeping watch in
a secure place where she knew she was safe, she'd call it
habit. She'd had to keep watch at night in the bar for so
long, it was hard to shake the habit. It would have been one of
her weaker lies, so she was quietly grateful nobody asked why
she sat just inside the balcony door, pipe in hand. She even had
some fresh tobacco, grown on a farm she'd never heard of.
Someone with a finer palate might have picked up flavors and
textures and all sorts of things she couldn't comprehend. For
Pickett, it was just a pleasant distraction.

Because she didn't stay awake out of habit, not anymore.
Months in the Elowey estate and coming home to find a third
person to share the night shifts with had more or less altered
the practice from what it had been before.

Sometimes things changed. Pickett glanced back to see Edie
on the cot. Merca had taken over the books when she retired,
but slept in her cozy room. But she left the cot in here. Had she
hoped Pickett would return? Had there been interim bookkeep-
ers? She hadn't thought to ask before Merca closed the door.
The room was different. There was a hideous painting of a glass

shark. Pickett had never seen one but some part of her knew it was ghastly. The shelves were organized differently. The desk had been shifted. Things changed.

So how would things change with Edie? Would it simply be her changing the pattern with the men she'd known? Or would things change between them, too?

She chewed on the lip of her pipe. The last time she'd been in this room, she'd believed in the myth of control over the change. She'd believed in things turning out well. And fuck, it hurt. She squeezed her eyes shut, focusing on the buzz of her pipe weed.

THEY ALWAYS KEPT one balcony door open in the night. Everything was hotter pressed up against another person, after all, and Pickett and Patr spent so much time pressed up against one another. At first, she wanted to relish every moment of it, so desperate to taste him and smell him and feel him she grew sick of his presence. That way, it wouldn't hurt so much when he eventually sailed away.

But he never sailed away. He stayed in Southfen, working this job or that, earning enough to keep a room at an inn and the occasional dinner. And Pickett never ever grew sick of him.

Her curves were modest, but he ran his hands over her, whispering his admiration in her ear. She seldom donned powders or rouge, but he caught his breath every time he saw her. When he was near, Pickett felt so, so beautiful.

It had been months since their first meeting as they lay on a blanket on the office floor, the cot being too small for them both, legs tangled and arms wrapped around each other. He pressed gentle kisses to her collarbone and whispered against her skin.

"There's an opportunity to make good money up north. I've been promised an apprenticeship keeping books in a noble house. It's better money than minding the logs for a sea captain. You do the same thing. You

could come with me. We could work together. Earn some money. Buy our own house."

Her own house. Pickett had never had a house. But suddenly that was all she wanted, a house and work and Patr. She didn't know her age. Merca thought she might be seventeen, but in that moment, Pickett felt twice as old and three times as wise as she hugged him close.

"Then we'll go north. Together."

EXCEPT "TOGETHER" had been all too temporary. A drunken ceremony in a temple for a god she didn't even remember. And then? The letter proved he had been alive at some point in the last few years. Who knew if that was still the case?

Pickett sighed and moved to refill her pipe when something moved in the corner of her eye. A figure? A shape? She leaned forward, but it seemed to disappear, blending into the crowd of drunken sailors. Maybe it had been something else entirely. Pickett shook her head and tapped out her pipe ash. She needed to stop fretting. She was only making matters worse.

With a sigh, she heaved herself to her feet and checked to see if she woke Edie. But no. Edie was still sleeping as peacefully here as she had back at the Pick's Pocket. She'd be gone for a day. Just a day. She'd go, she'd talk to a friend, and she'd be back. Edie wasn't Patr. Edie would come back.

Pickett locked the balcony door and decided, for once, she could trust that the Dames, or at least Merca, had her back, too. The past was the past. Time to sleep on it.

EIGHTEEN

Pickett jerked awake. For a moment, she wasn't sure why. Usually when she woke, it was either dawn or Edie coming in from her watch. But there was no light streaming in through the curtains, and Edie was next to her, only just twitching awake.

Pickett frowned, sitting up. There it was again. A clatter. And a thump.

"Edie," she hissed, shaking her awake. "Edie, get up. Someone's fucking around."

"Nngh, it's probably one of the dames," Edie groaned into her pillow.

"No, if there's anything a prostitute knows, it's how to sneak out quietly," Pickett whispered.

Another bang. Whoever it was, they were heading up the stairs. Pickett scrambled for the nearest weapon she could find, which was an abacus. She handed it to Edie and reached for her flints, slipping them onto her fingers. She could try scaring whoever it was, while Edie hit them over the head with a heavy calculating implement. It wouldn't be the first time Edie bashed in the head of an aggressor.

Another thump followed. It was growing closer by the second. Pickett clambered to her feet.

"Edie?"

"Got it," Edie said, all traces of drowsiness gone as she rose, brandishing the abacus like a mallet.

The door burst open. Edie swung the abacus at the figure, who ducked, shoving a different figure forward, this one bound like a pork roast. Pickett was ready to click her fingers together, perhaps even catch a lucky spark on the intruder's hair until, at last, her eyes adjusted and she saw them.

"Simon?" she gasped as Edie cried, "Jodiah!"

The bounty hunter shut the door behind him.

"You're a day early," Edie insisted. "We haven't figured out how to get Nancy out of the temple yet. Also, when the fuck were you going to tell me Nancy is Fistic's daughter?"

Jodiah all but growled as he glared down at Simon like he was some half-desiccated snake in the middle of the road. "I assume he was going to tell us at the same time he'd tell us he didn't actually have a plan to smuggle her out of the city."

Only then was Pickett able to grasp the situation in whole. There she and Edie were, and there the boys were. But Jodiah looked murderous with a knife clutched in one hand. And Simon lay in a heap on the floor, bound in ropes because he'd been caught. Her brother was back in her life and she'd let him lie to her again.

"Fuck," Pickett hissed. "Fuck you fucking fucker, what did you do?"

"He fucking played us is what he did," Jodiah snapped, hauling Simon up into a sitting position. "There we were, trying to obtain transport. Which he was supposed to do because he had all these resources available to him."

"It's more complicated—" Simon began to splutter, but Jodiah pressed a knife to his throat.

"We went to talk to his contacts. They turned him down.

Cold. We've got no ship, no carriage, not even a fruit cart to haul that girl out of here, because this man is a fucking liar. And I'm not excited to blaspheme without a proper payment!"

Jodiah shoved Simon with his boot, earning a grunt.

Simon begged. "Sonora!"

Pickett scowled, then stepped forward to shove Simon from the other side. "What the fuck is he talking about?"

Simon hung his head and wriggled, but he couldn't quite shake off Jodiah's skillful bindings. Pickett had to swallow back what threatened to transform into respect for the man.

"Fine," Simon muttered. He sucked in a deep breath then leaned back on his heels. He raised his chin, which might have seemed honorable except he focused more on her shoulders than her eyes. Fucking typical.

Pickett took a step back and crossed her arms. "Go on. Why the fuck didn't you fucking tell us?"

Simon gulped and shook his head. "Look. I was going to make sure you got your money. I swear. It doesn't matter what happened before."

"That's as helpful as toad spunk." Jodiah shoved Simon's shoulder with one foot. "Tell them everything."

Edie grasped Pickett's forearm. Simon hung his head, then raised it. This time, he only got as far as Pickett's navel.

"I met Nancy a few seasons ago," he muttered. "I wanted to propose. Things got complicated. I was liquidating assets. I was getting a ship. I was going to take her somewhere safe and I'd hire a guild protector like your friend here."

Pickett blinked once. Then twice. She tried to think straight but it was hard to string together a thought around the ringing in her ears. Simon was Nancy's lover. Her shit-brained brother had a shit-brained plan to steal the daughter of Southfen's most powerful businessman, and he'd made it their problem.

Jodiah wrinkled his nose and muttered something that even Pickett, with all her travels, had yet to hear. Pity. She'd have liked to take more time to appreciate that, except Simon was still fucking there. And she wanted so much to slam her boot into his nose. But there was Edie's hand on her arm, so she couldn't.

Pickett sucked in a sharp breath.

"What assets?" she demanded. "You told us someone hired you to hire us."

"To commit sacred crime," Jodiah added.

"To rescue a captive!" Edie snapped. "Pickett said so. Nancy doesn't want to be there."

"She doesn't." Simon wriggled against his bonds then sagged back. "Look. I want Nancy out of there. I-I'm the reason she's there. Her father didn't like me as a match. So I tried to make a fortune to impress him, but, you know, it can be complicated."

"For fuck's sake!" Jodiah raised the knife and pressed it into one of Simon's ears. In spite of herself, Pickett jumped forward. But Simon started on his own.

"I may have somewhat over-implied my current wealth value."

"He's broke," Jodiah said.

"Broke?" Pickett planted her hands on her hips. "I should have guessed it the second you showed your face in my bar. Would I be right to assume that there is nobody financing this little venture?"

"Yes and no-ah ah ah!" He jerked back as Jodiah began pressing the knife into his ear. "I have the money, all right! The person I'm working with is real. I swear to you on our mother and father's graves and the grave of that little frog you carried around in your pocket for a week. The benefactor is real. He paid for your room, not me. He's still in. Once we rescue her, he'll arrange for the transfer of the funds per our agreement. He wants her out of there as badly as I do."

Something about this felt wrong. Pickett leaned forward,

looking him up and down. "Why would some rich ass hire a man to rescue his own lover?"

Simon opened his mouth, then glanced up at Jodiah, then closed it and swallowed before he answered. "I don't know. But he approached me at a time when I really needed it. I-I took a risk. I needed to sell some goods fast, so I loaded all of it onto my ship. It was sailing across the Laughing Lake. I hired a captain who told me he knew the place."

"The Laughing Lake," Edie whispered, brows furrowing. "I swear I've heard of it."

"You probably heard about the big festival they had two and a half months ago outside Deep Knotting." Simon swallowed again. "Look, the captain told me it was safe. But he must have fucked up his dates, because he was doing it right during the Celebration of Joy. While everyone on the banks giggled from the lake gas, my whole crew died and the ship was scuttled on some rocks by the shore. Before I could even get to it, it was looted down to the last nail. It wasn't my fault. Honest! It was that captain's! He told me it would be just as safe on the lake as it was on land."

"Pity he can't pay for it," Jodiah growled. "So why would some fancy man hire a failed merchant to steal a captive from a temple."

"He didn't, exactly."

Fucking perfect. This was just making Pickett's skin crawl even more. Simon hung his head.

"I was drinking away my sorrows and I was approached by a man who bought me a drink. It led to another and another. I told him about Nancy and how I could never marry her now and he offered to help me. Even encouraged me to think about anyone else I could hire. He said if we were going against a runecrafter, I could use a witch on my side."

Edie muttered under her breath. Pickett wanted to snap or

scream or, really, have any sort of a huge response. But she just couldn't find it in herself. This was so fucking typical of him.

"Witch," Pickett repeated. "This man specifically used the word witch?"

Simon nodded. "And I hadn't thought about you in ages. But like I said, I knew about your bar the second word of it started floating around in trader circles. The man says witch and it occurred to me that I did know a witch, and it would be very nice to see her again. Maybe I could mend a bridge with you."

"So you not only lied about your fortune, you lied about the reason for bringing me on the job," she said dryly. There was a niggling discomfort in her chest that could turn into pain if she stopped to poke at it. She didn't. "Working with me wasn't even your idea. You can see that, right? Do you have enough of a brain to realize you were manipulated?"

Simon squirmed a little. "After how things left off between us, I couldn't just show up begging for help. And if you knew it was for my benefit, you might have said no on principle."

"Yes, I fucking would have. I fucking *should* have!" Pickett began to pace back and forth, pausing occasionally to shoot Simon a filthy look as she gathered her thoughts. Another miracle investor was involved in this mess, like the one who'd bought the Spotted Dick, like the one who had taken a shine to the Pick's Pocket. She spared Edie a look. In that moment she could tell, Edie was putting it together too.

"All of this happened two and a half months ago," Edie murmured. "It was only two months ago that Bresk reached out to me. Two miracle investors that close together doesn't feel like a coincidence, especially not when Simon was all but sent to us."

"Who is this friend of yours?" Pickett demanded, rounding on Simon. "Did you tell him about me?"

He glanced between them. "I said I might know a witch. But I never told him your name. Honest!"

Pickett couldn't even summon the name of a god to curse in that moment. She ran a hand over her face. "Why would you bring your troubles to me?" she spat. "Why? We haven't spoken in years!"

"Just because we were apart doesn't mean I didn't keep tabs on you. I lost track of you when you went up to Coldspine with that sailor, but when news of a bar called the Pick's Pocket started up in merchant circles, I thought to myself she's fine. She's back. Who else would name a bar that? And then I heard about everything with the swamp and the undead and how you used your magic to stop it." He began to tremble. "I promise, the job can still work out just fine. You'll still get your money. But please, don't turn me into something foul. I still want to be a good husband to Nancy."

"Wait," Edie cut in. "What did you mean by 'used her magic' just now?"

Simon sniffed, tears starting to brim in his eyes. "Everyone in Sedrios is talking about what happened in the Rottering swamp and I thought to myself if there was anyone who could save Nancy from a runecrafter, it was a swamp witch. And I was keeping tabs on you anyway, just to know you were alive. And he seemed surprised I had a magic sister and seemed interested, but I swear I didn't tell him your name."

"If he knows your name, he knows mine!" Pickett snapped. "Unless you at least used a false name? Please tell me you didn't . . ."

Simon's guilty expression said it all. Pickett pinched the bridge of her nose. "What were you thinking?"

"I was thinking I felt miserable. And I usually use a false name. Fistic thinks I'm Simon Porter, because Father had a bad reputation as an unreliable trader and I wanted to prove . . . I didn't think this fellow was actually going to be, I don't know, enough of a bother to hide it."

"And this friend of yours. Was he actually fool enough to think I could do magic?"

Simon sniffled, then blinked up at her. "Can't you?"

"I can't believe this," Jodiah muttered, finally jerking his knife back. "I was starting to think this was a setup, but it sounds like your brother really is that thick."

Frog-fucking feckless fucker.

"I can't do magic," she snarled. When Simon bobbed his mouth open, Pickett snatched her bag and started digging through it. "Do you see these? They're flints. I put them on my fingers and make sparks. And this?" She pulled out the blackout bottle. "Any stories about me making a room go black is because I smash this on the floor and the dust blocks the view. I don't have any more magic than you do."

"But-but the stories people tell."

"Because people will believe anything," Pickett snapped. "You really think I'd need your money if I could summon storms and everything else? I want people to believe that so they don't fuck with me."

"Sonora—"

"I can't listen to this anymore," Pickett muttered.

"On it," Edie said.

Before Simon could utter another word, Edie, absolute gem that she was, stuffed a rag in his mouth. He gagged, and she held up a finger.

"There we are. A few minutes of quiet to think," she said before turning back to Pickett and Jodiah. "Better?"

"Much," Pickett sighed.

Edie offered her a fleeting smile before she planted her hands on her hips. "So how are we all feeling about this?"

How was Pickett feeling? Lost. Confused. Angry. But those were normal. She could cycle through all of those feelings twice before breakfast. It had been a while since they'd been strong enough to make her feel like she could just fall right through the floor. Fucking Simon.

"I say we call off the job," Jodiah said.

"If we call it off, we risk upsetting a man rich enough to throw around a fortune to break Fistic's daughter out of a temple. I dunno what he's after but he made a deal with Simon and he's already got the bar."

"We don't know for certain it's the same rich guy," Edie insisted, but her words sounded brittle.

Pickett crossed her arms and arched a brow. "Right after Simon told his man about us, your friend shows up, pours money into it, and even gives you a magic pamphlet once Simon told him I was a witch. Edie, who have we heard of that's enough in competition with Fistic to throw around several suns just to screw him over?"

Edie clenched her jaw, staring hard at Pickett. The room went so quiet, the only sound was Simon's heavy breathing through his nose. Then the moment snapped like twine.

Edie dropped her arms, threw back her head, and shouted, "Cocks!"

CHAPTER

NINETEEN

"All right. New plan," Jodiah cut in. "We piss off back to the bar and forget the whole endeavor."

"Divine dickstains, Jodiah, we can't just fuck off," Pickett said, pinching the bridge of her nose. "The Gilt King's got his claws in the bar. He outright owns the Spotted Dick. Even if we try to piss off, he'll just show up again and drag us into it."

"Well then I'll piss off on my own and drink myself half to death in your precious bar!" Jodiah snapped, stomping toward the door.

"Did you not hear the part where Nancy is imprisoned against her will?" Pickett demanded. "Magically imprisoned, I might add."

"Why do you care? She's not your fiancé," Jodiah threw over his shoulder.

Edie jumped in front of the door, arms crossed.

"The real question is why don't you care?" Edie demanded. "Would a man who fears the wrath of Al-Dagos really turn his back on an aberration like this?"

Jodiah scowled. "Don't you dare—"

"I have read the meditations of the right and virtuous traveler Isfaley," Edie said, raising her chin with just the hint of a smirk. "I was a milkmaid once. It's boring work. I read every scrap of paper that came through my town and every one that came through the bar, too. Not that the bar is boring." She smiled faintly at Pickett.

Jodiah's fingers twitched, but he didn't reach for his crossbow.

"For the deities who walk our lands and swim our seas, who fly through our air and turn time and purpose inside and out, the natural balance of the world can surely be to them as bread is to us."

"Don't," Jodiah growled.

"The natural balance to those who govern our world must be beyond our senses. Those ideas which are ephemeral to mortals are solid to gods. Virtue. Vision. And, above all, justice."

Edie arched a brow. "Wouldn't you say removing corruption and scandal like this from a temple is justice?"

Jodiah twitched his fingers, but he didn't quite ball them into fists.

"What exactly do you need from me then?" he growled.

Edie grinned. "Well to start, I need to go back to the bar. You watch my back, and we'll be back in just a day. Then we can decide how to help Nancy without playing into the Gilt King's hands."

The thought made Pickett's gut flip. "Edie, don't you think we can figure this out now?"

Edie only shook her head. "If Bresk is really the Gilt King, then I'd really rather be careful. Let's not rush into anything. For all we know, this may still end with us in the middle of a commerce war."

Simon wriggled against his restraints and grunted through his gag. Pickett rolled her eyes and tugged it down.

"We don't need to fight the Gilt King," Simon insisted. "He's helping me to get my beloved. He's a friend."

"Really? What's his name?" Pickett demanded.

Simon opened his mouth, then shut it fast enough to make his teeth click.

"You see?" Pickett scoffed. "He's doing it for his own gain. Stealing away the daughter of his great rival? It's nowhere near charity."

"Exactly," Edie said, but there was a flush to her cheeks and a shake to her hands. Good fuck. Was she embarrassed she'd fallen for the Gilt King's crap, too? It would be adorable if not for the situation they were in.

"How do we save the girl?" Jodiah snapped, then he spun toward Pickett. "I doubt the gods will be pleased to see us smack against a wall when they realize your ass of a brother doesn't have a way to smuggle her out. If he did, I have no doubt this Gilt King would know about it."

"Simple." Pickett pressed her hands to her chest and shrugged. "I am not Simon. I'm not even Edie. I don't know this Gilt King as far as I'm aware. That means I'm free to remove impediments from our path."

"How?"

Pickett swept back her colorful, runed cape and dipped into a bow. "By not doing whatever the fuck Simon was planning. Maybe I can even convince her not to marry him and solve everybody's problem, but the main goal is to get her the fuck out of there."

"Sonora!" Simon gasped, but Pickett refused to so much as look at him.

"I'll take care of getting us transportation and keeping Simon on a leash," she continued. "Edie, are you sure going back to the bar is wise? If this consult of yours is with Hoag, you can just say so. I won't judge you for taking advice from him."

"It's not."

Somebody yelled in the halls, followed by the stomp of feet. Pickett barely had time to slip her flints on before the door slammed open, revealing an enraged Merca. Her hair was bound in a beautiful silken scarf. Her face was stripped of any sort of cosmetic being instead caked here and there with different-colored clays, each no doubt having its own beauty secret. Fuck, even now she was beautiful. If Pickett allowed herself to care how she looked, she might actually be jealous.

"My girl," Merca said, her tone wavering between calm control and rage. "You know you are welcome here, but my people work late hours. The last thing they need is screaming and slamming when they're trying to catch up on their . . ." She broke off, glancing first at Jodiah, then at Simon, brows furrowed. Right. She would have only met him the one time back when he'd ditched Pickett here as a girl.

"I'm sorry, Merca," Pickett ground out. "We'll keep it down. Jodiah, take Simon out to the hall."

Jodiah groaned, but went to untie Simon's bonds.

"Fuck it, bounty hunter, just drag him out!"

"Sonora!"

Jodiah hesitated, then grinned and grabbed Simon by his wrists, dragging him out bit by agonizing bit. Merca grunted, clearly not impressed as she shot Pickett one more warning look, then slipped back out. It was only when the door shut behind them that Pickett dropped all semblance of confidence and squeezed Edie's hands.

"I thought we agreed no more secrets," she said. "This makes for two new buddies you haven't introduced me to, and the first one is probably the Gilt King."

"I promise this one isn't like the investor." Edie laughed, but it was little more than a short, swift bark, and she sobered all too soon. "His name is Skilp. He's . . . It's hard to explain. It'll be better to just introduce you in person, which I'll do when this is all over. I promise."

"Edie, I don't want you to leave me." The words slipped out before she could stop them. Pickett's heart twisted. Her cheeks burned. She clenched her teeth and squeezed Edie's hands all the tighter. "Just stay."

"I'll be back before you know it," Edie insisted.

"You've got your stupid pamphlet."

"A stupid, limited, hand-drawn pamphlet," Edie pointed out. "Provided by someone we don't trust. I'd like a second opinion, Pickett. I have a chance to help this girl the way I know we both want to. Why not let me try?"

"Because . . ." Because why? If Edie failed, they'd have to resort to a more barbaric method one way or another. Because she didn't want to do the job alone? Poor excuse. She'd met Nancy alone last time and found out about the runes and Corsa's skill set.

Because.

"Simon ditched me when I was a child," she said. "He wasn't the only one. I met someone while I was here, too. Someone I loved. Then I lost him. And maybe it's ridiculous but I don't want to lose you, too."

Edie blinked slowly, then smiled. She pressed a hand to Pickett's cheek.

"I'm just going to the bar and back," she said softly. "You won't lose me. There's nowhere in the world I would rather be than by your side."

"That's not—"

"Pickett!" Edie stepped forward. "I'm not them. Any of them. I'm the milkmaid who killed a dangerous brute in your bar to save her own skin. And you protected me. You gave me a home. Do you think someone like me would shy away from that?"

Pickett didn't know what answer to provide. There was Edie. Edie who knew how to charm their customers. Edie who could cook. Edie who did, indeed, read everything she could get her hands on. Who trusted people. Who loved people. Edie who turned a broken-down bar into a home.

"Trust me," Edie pleaded. "If we want to save this girl and figure out who's meddling with us, then I need to do this."

IN THE END, Pickett really had no choice. They made the arrangements and speculated on when to plan for Edie and Jodiah's return. All Pickett wanted was to hold her close and forbid her to leave. But she didn't. Trust felt like a bloodletting.

Pickett stood on the balcony, watching Edie shrink into a speck in the distance, Jodiah looming over her like a raincloud. It was almost dawn. They'd be at the bar by mid-morning. Depending on how long it took Edie to find her friend and get answers, they'd probably be back some time in the early evening.

Edie would come back. Pickett just had to keep reminding herself that Edie would come back.

Simon sat at the desk that used to be hers, rubbing his fingers over the worn grain.

"You're sure Edie can find a way to free Nancy?" he asked.

"I'm sure she's our best chance." Pickett pulled out her pipe and bag of leaf and sank into the chair opposite him. Maybe the pleasant fog of a good smoke would ease the squirming in her gut.

Simon sighed, tapping his fingers, then leaning back to run his hands through his hair. Had he always been this fidgety? Pickett honestly couldn't remember. As a child, he'd always looked so great. Now he was just an anxious fool wiggling like a worm on the boardwalk.

Pickett tapped some of the leaf into the bowl. "What was your plan for her runes, anyway?"

Simon laughed wryly and scratched his chin. "No plan. I never thought Fistic would resort to something that would hurt her."

"I guess people can surprise you." Pickett snapped her flints a few times until the leaf caught, then bit down on the pipe. In seconds, the scorching-sweet scent filled the room. Pickett could relax.

Simon wrinkled his nose. "When did you pick up smoking?" he asked.

"Sometime after you dropped me off here."

And there was the anxious tapping again. If she tied his hands together, would he turn to tapping his feet? Hard to say what would be more annoying.

"You know I left you here because they'd take care of you," he pointed out. "Merca promised me you'd be fine. You were fed, they taught you numbers, put you to work in the office."

"One man's sheepdog is another man's cur."

"You're not a cur," Simon said softly. Then, in what Pickett could only assume was an afterthought, he added, "You look nice."

"You can save the compliment for Merca."

Simon sighed and shifted in his seat. "Fine. In the meantime, what's the plan? If Edie can find a way to get rid of Nancy's runes, we still need transportation out of the city."

"Simple." Pickett took a long pull from the pipe, let the buzz fill her mouth, then puffed out a perfect smoke ring. "You turn me in."

CHAPTER

TWENTY

Why did rope have to be so scratchy? In a world of water mills and crossbows and other technological wonders, why didn't anyone ever get around to inventing less scratchy rope. It would certainly make the bounty hunter's guild more popular with their targets.

"Couldn't we have done this some other way?" Simon asked as they walked up the winding road to the Elowey house.

Pickett glanced behind her. Simon was dressed in some of Jodiah's leather armor, but no amount of cinching and adding on knives could make him look like he wasn't, well, Simon.

"You didn't offer a different plan," Pickett snapped.

Simon glanced to the side then back at her. "I look ridiculous. I look like a fishmonger dressing up. How does anyone wear this armor? I'm boiling alive."

"I don't know. How does someone ditch a relative in a brothel?" Pickett snapped.

She glared down at the road in front of her. Behind her, Simon sighed.

"I can keep justifying why Merca was better equipped to take care of you than I was," he muttered. "I was a child, too."

"We could have been children together."

"They didn't have room for me there. Not really." Simon slowed, and Pickett had to pick up her own pace, half-dragging him with her ropes to keep them from looking too suspicious.

"Would you care to stop whining about the consequences of your old actions?" she demanded. "If you're not going to apologize properly, then I don't want to hear it."

Simon sighed. "Fine. Care to remind me why I'm necessary for your charade?"

"Because on my own they'd frisk me, take the comb, and boot me back out," Pickett said. "With you, they get to gloat that I was caught, which means we'll have them as an audience."

"Charming." They stopped at the door, and Simon slammed the knocker a few times. Pickett glanced over her shoulder. There was Southfen, looking like a toy town next to the sea. And beyond? Edie was out in the woods beyond the buildings. No time to focus on her just yet.

The door opened and there was Spidernose, regarding both of them with casual disdain. At least, until he truly took Pickett in.

"You," he snarled.

Picket raised her bound wrists and wiggled her fingers at me. "Me. And him." She nodded at Simon.

Spidernose glanced between the two of them, brows furrowed, before he stepped aside, pulling the door a little wider. "Come on in, then. Lady Elowey will be thrilled at the return of her property. Perhaps even enough to offer a reward." He offered Simon a small, tight smile before turning on his heel to march down the hall. Simon followed behind him, mincing his steps as he glanced around at the opulence of the fine house.

"Never been somewhere this . . ." He wrinkled his nose and closed his mouth. "Am I tracking dirt? This is rude. I'm being rude, aren't I?"

Clearly, Simon had never gone far as a merchant, even before the Laughing Lake.

"Doesn't matter. Someone'll be by to clean it soon." Pickett leaned a little closer and grinned. "Sometimes, if they're having a bad day, they just spit on the floor while they do it. Just to express themselves. Like artists but with substandard cleaning."

Simon made a face, but Spidernose called over his shoulder. "That is a vicious rumor I happen to know you started!"

She hadn't, but there was no point in trying to convince him of that.

Lady Elowey sat in the library, lounging on a settee, a book in hand. She arched a brow at Simon, then crossed one slippered foot over the other.

"Hidge, give this man a few shims and a fresh waterskin for his trouble."

Simon sputtered. "Well, that's not exactly—"

"Fine," she sighed. "A silver scale. Hidge, did you get my comb back from her?"

"Not yet, mistress," Spidernose said.

She scoffed and closed her book, tilting her head in his direction. Before he could say another word, Pickett stepped forward.

"Rather than go through the discomfort of a frisking, I'll just give it to you," she said. "I guarantee if he looks, he won't find it."

Lady Elowey blinked slowly at her, then gestured to Spidernose. He scowled and cracked his knuckles, before patting Pickett down. With each pocket that failed to produce the comb, however, he began to dig through with more desperation, locating her blackout bottles, some coins, and—her cheeks burned—the letter, which joined a growing pile on the floor.

"What's taking so long, Hidge?"

"I told you. I'll give it to you."

Lady Elowey lolled her head to the side and frowned. "And

what advantage is it to you to just hand over the comb? If we don't find it, you can proclaim your innocence."

Pickett grinned. "Fistic sold you my shit contract. He wasn't cutting you a good deal, and we both know it, at least now. Are you interested in perhaps ruining his day?"

Elowey stared at her for a long moment before, with a little twitch of her wrist, she sent Spidernose scurrying back.

"Explain," she said icily.

"I will. But first . . ." She twisted her wrists, loosening the slip knots holding her bonds in place. Simon coiled the rope up and slipped it into his day pack. Lady Elowey's expression soured all the more.

"Right." Pickett gestured to herself. "We both know I'm a crap servant. You must not be happy with him after hiring me."

"Mm," Elowey hummed, tapping a finger on her book. "He sold your contract to me for a suspiciously low rate."

"I'm also willing to guess that, if you and Fistic aren't friends, then you might just be friends with his rival, the Gilt King." Pickett grinned. "I mean, he's bought up half of South-fen, hasn't he? Why not buy off one of its wealthiest residents?"

"Ah. It looks like your short time back in the world has taught you so much," Elowey said. She sat up straighter, finally setting her book aside. "What do you know about the Gilt King?"

"As much as anyone knows about a gilded tiara. Pretty on the outside but uncertain of what lies beneath."

"Mm. You should be singing his praises," Elowey said. "I was ready to sell you to pirates after you damaged my hair. He interceded on your behalf and convinced me to keep you on. He even promised someone else would buy your contract so I wouldn't be stuck with you for your whole term." She leaned forward, resting her chin in one hand. "Why would the new richest man in this part of Sedrios be so interested in you?"

Why indeed? The timelines were adding up. He'd bought the

Spotted Dick and, somewhere around that time, he'd met Simon and concocted the scheme to pull Nancy out of the temple. Then he'd gone to Edie. He'd given her a pamphlet of runes and invested in fixing up the bar, which meant he probably knew runes himself. Fuck, he'd probably been the one to suggest she invest her new profits in getting Pickett out of her servitude early. He was a shitty, horrid, manipulative, magical piece of diseased donkey shit, and they were all playing in his dung heap.

Simon wiped his brow. Pickett forced herself to smile.

"You didn't hear? I am the witch of the Rottering swamp. Perhaps you've heard of my establishment. The Pick's Pocket?"

Spidernose swore and jumped back, making a gesture against evil.

"Charming," Elowey said dryly. "But I doubt he's in need of your services."

"On the contrary. He's hired us indirectly to do a job for him. One which will certainly deal a blow to Fistic."

Elowey's eyes sparkled and she grinned, taking on that same hungry quality Pickett had seen so many times in Fistic's eyes. Whatever power games were going on between Fistic and the Gilt King, Elowey was involved. The sooner they got Nancy away from these people, the better.

"Either you're being paid very well or you have a lot of anger for Fistic."

"Why can't it be both?" Pickett shrugged. "I'll give you your comb and a chance to humiliate an enemy of yours. And all I need is a ship."

Spidernose barked out a laugh. "You overestimate my lady's anger."

"Not a big ship," Simon snapped at him. "And not to keep. We'd just borrow it."

"Just enough to get her out of the Southfen harbor," Pickett added. "Helm it with your men and all they have to do is drop us and the girl off somewhere else. It'll cost you nothing."

"Nothing costs nothing," Elowey purred.

"Maybe not," Pickett agreed before reaching into Simon's pocket and procuring the comb. "But sticking it to Fistic will cost you a ship for a night or two."

Elowey's eyes widened and Spidernose snatched it out of Pickett's hand, glaring at her as he handed it to Elowey. She took it and made to put it in her hair before peering closely at the bristles and handing it back to Spidernose.

"Have that cleaned," she instructed. "And as for you? You get no ship. You get a cart and a mule, and you will be grateful I haven't decided to imprison you."

Pickett dipped into a bow. "Your magnanimity is legendary, Lady Elowey."

"As is your audacity." Elowey arched a brow. "Next time you hire someone to impersonate a bounty hunter, perhaps look further than the nearest fish market? He looks ridiculous."

TWENTY-ONE

S o you say you've uncovered my enemy."

The absolute picture of leisure and arrogance, Pickett ran her fingers over the soft fabric of Fistic's chair. At least she hoped she pulled off the confident effect she strived for. She just had to impersonate the man in front of her. Calm. Arrogant. She could be the poor version of Fistic. This part would be easier since, with Simon back at the Spotted Dick, she could focus entirely on the con. If Fistic was in the city when they broke Nancy out, then Corsa might be able to inform Fistic before they escaped. He'd be able to lock that girl away for good and Pickett couldn't let that happen.

Fortunately, she'd finally learned what might drive him to abandon sense and reason: Nancy and Simon. If he believed Simon was at the heart of all of this, there was a good chance she could get him out of the way long enough to smuggle Nancy out of the city. It all depended on her selling this with unwavering confidence.

"I've learned a little about the Gilt King," Pickett said.

Fistic slipped a few seeds into the cage of one of his birds, his lips pursed. Of all the times Pickett had been in this office, she'd never really thought about the cages. Then again, of all the times she'd been in this office, she'd never known Fistic would put his own daughter in one.

The moment stretched on, and Pickett was tempted to break it, but the purse of his lips suggested that might be unwise. Once his pets began pecking at their food, he pulled back, smoothing over his moustache before turning to her.

"Do you have a name?"

Pickett shrugged. "I've heard he goes by Bresk, but it's probably another fake. It's the name he used when he spoke to my kitchen girl."

Fistic wiped some of the dust from the seeds onto a handkerchief and set it on his desk. The birds squawked in their cages, happily gnawing on their treats as he turned away from them, sinking into his own plush chair. His handsome face was schooled into a careful, neutral expression. A long moment passed before he finally heaved a heavy sigh.

"I see. You offer an unhelpful false alias and the knowledge that he has played you and your girl as well as half of Southfen. With everything else he's done, the knowledge that he'd expand into the swamp is not surprising and hardly worth the value of restructuring a major infrastructure project and diverting business. You ask ten times the effort from me that you're willing to put in yourself."

"And what sort of a friend would I be if that's really all I had to offer?" Pickett leaned forward. "I know about some of the actions he's taking in Southfen. And what he's doing right now."

"Besides trying to buy out every business I've carefully fostered relationships with?" Fistic drummed his fingers on his desk.

Pickett grinned. She'd found the best time to twist the game was when someone was unamused. "You're right. He's definitely doing that. But he's also doing a little charitable work.

You see, I came to town because I was hired to bust someone out of the temple of Al-Dagos. Lovely girl. Patroness. Holy virgin, I hear."

The drumming stopped and, with it, the conversation. That was fine. Pickett knew how to pick it up again. Time to twist this for him.

"A young man named Simon Porter hired us."

For the first time since she'd met him, Pickett could say the money lender looked openly upset. No veneer of pleasantness or scheming. No. He looked like someone whose lunch was just starting to disagree with him. Good. Clearly, he was buying it, which meant he didn't know what a stonebrain her brother could be.

"Then you came at the whim of a fool to complete an impossible task," Fistic growled.

"Probably." Pickett shrugged. "Thing is, Simon has a soft spot for me, being my brother and all."

Fistic's mouth visibly fell open, enough that she could probably toss a pip into it if she wanted to. She grinned and carried on.

"That's right. It's not Simon Porter; it's Simon Pickett. It also turns out this Gilt King has bought the brothel I grew up in. He's also invested in the Pick's Pocket. Who else would do that but a doting brother hoping to reconnect with his sister?"

"Nonsense," Fistic spat. "I had word Simon invested everything in a doomed ship."

"And how convenient," Pickett mused. "Nobody would look at a man like him and think he was the master investor set on taking over Southfen."

Fistic's lip curled. "Lies."

Lies were more effective if there was truth tied into them. "Maybe. Or maybe he offered me half a golden sun if I could help him bust Nancy out of that little temple."

Fistic slammed his fist on his desk so hard he knocked over

his candles, the wet wax killing the flame and spreading out over the wood. In their cages, the birds squawked and protested. Pickett had to bite back a grin. At the moment, Fistic definitely hated two people: Simon and the Gilt King. For one of them, he might be willing to play into a plot. For both of them wrapped in a convenient package? Even a clever man could be blinded.

Fistic leaned forward on the desk, his hungry eyes positively burning. "And I suppose you think it's wise to cross me."

Pickett rested her chin in one hand and shrugged. "I said he wanted to pay me that. I didn't say I actually wanted in on any of his schemes."

Fistic looked ready to slam his fist down again. Then a serene expression overtook his face. He relaxed, leaning back into his chair as he considered Pickett thoughtfully. "So why tell me any of this?"

"You must have guessed," Pickett said. "Simon thinks we have far more love between us than we actually do. He abandoned me when I was wee—in a brothel. He can get stuffed, and I'd like to have a hand in the stuffing."

Fistic hummed and leaned back in his seat. "So what else are you hoping to gain from me? Southfen has no formal law enforcement. And it strains credulity to believe that even you would want me to have him killed, if indeed that is your plan."

Pickett sighed heavily and shrugged. "I suppose I can't very well do that. There's probably some god or spirit out there who punishes the killing of a brother. But he abandoned me. I can hardly bear to see him make off as happy as the moon is bright at the expense of a good friend of mine. So here's what I suggest. For a minimal charge." Pickett leaned forward, looking at the spilled wax. It looked a bit like water. She plucked a few seeds out of Fistic's bowl of bird treats. "If I am correct and Simon is, in fact, the Gilt King, then him marrying your daughter puts him in a position to take it all from you. Either now or when you meet your sweet hereafter. And neither of us wants that. Plus, if he succeeds in getting to Nancy, he wins. Which we also do not want."

She began setting the seeds on the wax.

"Let us suppose the impossible is made possible by a rival with a lot of resources. Let us suppose there is actually a way to pull Nancy from her safe haven. The most practical way for our star-crossed lover is by boat, obviously. He plans to spirit her out to sea at dusk."

"Simple, I'll have a ship intercept them."

"And that would work." Pickett shrugged. "But suppose they see you of all people standing at the bow." She moved one seed to face the others. "They wouldn't dare cross with you there. You could summon a whole fleet, and however lovestruck she is, I doubt your girl would allow his ship to attack yours. Either they retreat back to Southfen where some of your enforcers could be waiting to escort Simon here, where you negotiate a truce before the commerce war starts. Or"—she plucked the seed that was Simon's imaginary ship out of the wax—"he sees you making way and doesn't attempt to sail out at all. He'll be trapped in the port. Then it's a simple matter of catching them when they're forced back onto land."

Fistic began to stroke his moustache with one thumb.

"Sounds like a waste of an evening. I've been assured Nancy can't leave."

"Oh?" Pickett leaned in close. "Some sort of magic assistance keeping her in place? Keeping her bound?"

"What?" Fistic wrinkled his nose. "I'll hire a rune woman, but none of that nonsense is ever to touch Nancy."

Well. That was unexpected. Pickett opened her mouth, half tempted to tell him about the mark on Nancy's arm, then stopped herself. The goal was to keep him from meddling with Nancy's escape. If he found out, he'd probably barge into the temple himself to confirm the news. Nancy's rune would remain a mystery for another day, but it was nice to know she could hate Fistic a little less than she had before. It didn't mean she was going to back off on busting Nancy out, though.

"Well," she said instead. "Supposing he finds a way past the runecrafter, I'm sure you'll enjoy humiliating him during his escape. They'll call you Fistic the Uncrossable or something like that. The man who broke the Gilt King. Saved his daughter. Real song-worthy shit."

Fistic grunted. "Explain to me why, precisely, I can't simply send my men to collect your brother now?"

"Because I don't actually know where he is," Pickett lied with a little shrug. "Nor how he plans to bust your little bird out. Just where he plans to be and when."

"And you have chosen to pass this information along to me," Fistic said. "But I assume you have an additional price?"

Pickett shrugged. "For the information I bring today? Only the continued warmth of our shared love for each other. Well, that and ensuring the new road favors my bar. And of course, when all of this is over, toss some chum back to an old friend. Whatever the chaos, I come out of this with my bar and the Spotted Dick still standing. But mostly the shared love and friendship and all that."

Fistic snorted and stared down at the mess of wax and seeds.

"This plan only really works if they try to escape by sea. If you're as estranged as you say, perhaps your brother wouldn't tell you about a change in plans."

"That's why you find the one place that rents carriages out. Put one of your men at the reins. Have him deliver them right back here. Safe and . . ." Pickett faltered, remembering the blood welling on Nancy's arm. Blood from a rune Fistic might not have been responsible for. She swallowed and forced a sickly smile. "Safe and sound. It's a backup. If Simon tries to escape by carriage, you have him held here so you can return and humiliate him in your office instead."

"And if they try to leave on foot?" Fistic muttered, picking up the seed. "You suggest I spare enforcers to guard every way in and out of Southfen. Not to mention the ones I'll have to send to the front of the temple."

"Simon's scrawny. It won't take many of your men to subdue him," Pickett pointed out. "And sure, you'll stretch things thin, but won't it be delightful to make your daughter see once and for all what an ass of a lover she's chosen? It might just be enough to put her off him altogether." Pickett jumped up from her seat and extended a hand. "Well, Mr. Fistic? Do we have an agreement? Fuck over the Loverboy and disenchant the swooning maiden? Come on. Won't it be fun to get your hands dirty for once?"

Fistic stared at her hand. A hungry grin spread across his face.

"Perhaps I truly can call you friend," he mused, taking her hand.

TWENTY-TWO

Pickett sat on the balcony once again. Merca had come and gone. Lunch had come and gone. Edie was still just gone.

Simon sat, legs pulled up to his chest. "You were right, Nora. We've got Fistic out of the way, we've got a cart coming from the Eloweys. All we need is your girl and this might just work."

"More or less," Pickett muttered. Staring at the street wasn't going to make Edie move any faster, but that didn't stop Pickett from trying.

Simon was quiet for a blessed few minutes before he spoke up again. "Edie is your girl, isn't she? You seem awfully attached to her. The way I am to Nancy."

The way he was to Nancy. That was more of a punch to the gut than it should have been. Pickett fiddled with her flints.

"Not like that," she muttered. "I've been married. It didn't take."

"It couldn't hurt to try again."

"Why do you care?" she snapped, shooting a glare his way.

Simon met her gaze and, for once, there was no squirming or fiddling. He sat perfectly still, his voice perfectly even.

"I care because I know we're both trying to build the same thing," he said. "We just want a home. I hate to see you turning away because of what I or anyone else did, Sonora. You deserve better than that."

"I deserve a stiff drink when this is over. That's what I deserve."

Simon smiled wanly and pushed himself to his feet. "I'll go ask Merca to set one aside for us."

He left, shutting the door silently behind him. Pickett doubted there'd be a bottle of anything at the end of this for the two of them. If there was, it would be for him and his new bride. That was fine. Pickett didn't need him in her life. If Nancy was free and he was gone, that would be enough for her.

And yet, there was still that scrap of paper in her pocket, heavy as an anchor.

Pickett sighed and pulled out the letter. After riding around in her pocket for so long, it was wrinkled and creased. Maybe she should have read it right away. Maybe she shouldn't read it at all.

"Fuck it all," she muttered, breaking the seal to unfold it. The sight of that familiar handwriting made her heart thud. How many times had she watched Patr writing letters to potential employers or draft flyers to post in taverns offering their services?

My dearest Pickett,

It has been so long since I saw your face, and its absence leaves my world all the darker. I regret that I left you so long. I regret changing my plan and not informing you. I can only imagine your worry when I did not return on time. So it is fitting that, when I did return, you were not there. I promised to protect you and I failed.

I am still determined as ever to make something great of myself and to provide for you the golden life you deserve. I know I have

*worn my name thin with my many insufficient endeavors, but I will
find a way to rectify my past mistakes. You will know me, my truest
love, by the name I take from the tavern where I left you. I wear it as
a chain to remind me of my mistakes and what I have to fight for.*

*I trust Merca will deliver this to you at her earliest convenience.
She was always kind to us.*

Know that you are forever in my heart.

Your husband,

Patr

Good to know he regretted leaving her. Didn't leave her any
less left. So what was he going by? Patr Shitty-Bar? Patr Creaky-
Floorboards? How could she not even remember the name of
the tavern?

She ought to crumple up the letter, go downstairs, and toss it
in the fire. And yet Pickett folded it up all the same, slipping it
back into her pocket. It was nice, sometimes, to remember when
someone wanted her enough to marry her. But now she had the
bar. She had Edie. Patr and Simon and soon this whole adventure could settle in her past. She could remember bits of it
fondly, sure. But nothing more. It was time to move on.

TWENTY-THREE

For better or worse, more than likely worse, Pickett slipped on a dark, hooded cloak to wait in the alley just outside the temple. It was half to hide her face and half to hide the runed cloak she still had on underneath. There wasn't a god or king who could convince her to face Corsa without it. Not that it was likely to matter. Edie and Jodiah were still gone.

The sun slid low, casting the whole of Southfen in a golden-pink light. Sweat slid down the back of Pickett's neck. The last service of the day was about to occur. Either they went in now or the plan was off.

Simon sidled up beside her, his face hidden by a wide-brimmed, straw hat. "Fistic's ship left port," he whispered. "Not sure if he's on it but if you sold him as well as you say, then this might just work. I just checked around the corner. If Elowey's cart is waiting for us, then all we need is Nancy."

And Edie. Pickett fiddled with her flints and had to force herself not to check her pockets, just to reassure herself that she had her blackout bottles on her. With how things were going so far, she'd pull them out to check them and wind up smashing them on the ground. This whole mission was still so fucked. Pickett glanced over her shoulder. Still no Edie. One of these days, she would have to buy a damned orven so they could keep in contact at times like this.

The deep toll of the evening prayer bell donged through the town. Clearly, not many people in Southfen were interested in praying to a wisdom goddess because only a handful of supplicants shuffled in, dropping coins and shells into a bucket held by a pauldroned patroness. Damn. If she'd realized they accepted other payment, she'd have visited the beach. Too late now, and not just for the payment.

"Let's go back to the Spotted Dick. I'll hire a messenger to send the cart back without us."

"What?" Simon grabbed her arm and spun her around to face him fully. "No. Fistic's looking the other way. We have a cart. We have to go tonight!"

"It doesn't matter," Pickett snapped. "Edie's not here. Without her, we don't know how to get Nancy out of there safely."

"There's no way that rich woman would offer us transportation again."

"Then we find another way, Simon," Pickett said. "Nancy has runes that will slice into her arm if she tries to leave. And I don't think Fistic is responsible, so this is even more complicated. Also maiming the bride is hardly going to be a good way to start a marriage."

Simon gritted his teeth and growled out, "I'm not leaving without her."

"Sometimes you have to abandon the plan." Pickett jerked her arm back. "Since when did you have a problem with taking off?"

Simon narrowed his eyes and opened his mouth before sprinting toward the temple. Fuckmongers!

Pickett pulled the hood low over her face and fell into the

crowd, shoving past the fishmongers and messengers and who-the-fuck-knew-what as Simon bobbed and swerved, darting around the back. She ducked low, narrowly missing a large basket of fruit someone was carrying, and tried to follow, just in time for one of the elderly patronesses to block her path, ringing a bell to summon any worshippers to the evening prayers. Pickett hissed under her breath, but the old bint was blocking the alley. She had to find the imbecile before he ruined everything. Pickett struggled to keep her hood low on her face as she pivoted, heading for the main entrance. The tithe bucket materialized in front of her.

"This is why most people don't like to go to the fucking temple," she snarled, dropping a pip in before pulling her hood down low enough to satisfy their weird religious rules.

Pickett scurried through the cool halls and into the prayer room with the great dragon statue. As she turned to look around, she couldn't spot a straw hat, just hoods and veils and the usual. Nor did she see any apprentice patronesses in the back with Nancy's full figure. Balls, where had they gone?

An elderly patroness shuffled to the front of the room then raised her shaking hands.

"The evening devotional," she announced, then paused. "You there. Sit down."

"Um"—Pickett glanced around—"sorry. I need a chamber pot. Don't want to focus more on my gut than the goddess. You understand. Don't worry, I'll find one myself. Maybe pop home and head back."

Scandalized whispers rose up from the room. Yet as Pickett backed out, nobody tried to stop her. As she slipped back into the hall, a low, guttural song started up from the room, followed by a humming crowd. If the evening prayer was as short as the midday one, there wasn't much time.

Pickett darted through the halls, shoving her head in room after empty room.

"Simon," she called as loud as she dared, checking a closet with brooms, then another with scrolls. The humming of the prayer still echoed through the whole temple but, as she turned down one of the dark halls, another sound cut through it.

Moaning.

For fuck's sake.

Pickett kicked open the door. The room was little bigger than a closet, but there were two cots squeezed against either wall with just enough room for a small chest of drawers with a pitcher and basin atop them. In one of the cots lay a pair of lovers in the process of removing each others' clothes.

Simon yelped. Nancy shrieked and pulled her dress back up over her shoulder.

"I take it this isn't the first time he's been to see you," Pickett drawled, crossing her arms. "Tell me, did you really hire me because you missed me or because you thought a swamp witch could get rid of her rune?"

"I . . ." Simon cleared his throat. "Well she didn't tell me it would hurt her, I didn't realize . . ."

"Simon thought he knew a way to get me out," Nancy offered weakly.

"And I see your clothes were detrimental to your escape," Pickett remarked.

Simon wrapped his arms around Nancy and shot her a grin. "I haven't seen her in half a year. You wanted me to just walk away from my betrothed?"

"Until we knew for sure we could get her out of here? Yes!" Pickett snapped. "And you! Ignoring the fact that holy virgins shouldn't take absolute imbeciles to bed in the temple, where's your watchdog?"

"Corsa's on an errand," Nancy muttered as she smoothed back a few wayward curls.

"And do you know when she'll be back?" Pickett demanded.

Nancy shrugged. Either she was perfect for Simon or love

just had a way of draining the sense out of anyone who fell into it.

"Well I'm breaking up this little rendezvous," she said. "Simon, tie up your breeches. We're going."

"Why the hurry?" a voice purred in the dark. Pickett whirled around to see the shadows on the wall just outside the room shifting to reveal Corsa's wicked grin.

"Good fuck, were you hiding in the shadows?" Pickett yelped.

"Taking a little nap until I heard a familiar voice," Corsa said, pushing forward to stand fully in the hall, the lingering dark falling like smoke from around her skirts. "It's hard to know what's going on in a shadow, but you've got a way of grating the ears. I must say, when Fistic told me to play along with whatever you were doing, I thought for sure—"

She stiffened. Her eyes went wide as she looked over Pickett's shoulder. Pickett turned to see Simon staring back at her with the same shocked expression.

"You're not supposed to be here," she snarled.

Nancy scrambled to her feet, glancing between them with about as much confusion as Pickett felt. "Simon, do you know her?"

"I-I do, darling," Simon breathed. "But she doesn't work for your father. She works for—"

Corsa screamed and waved her hands through the air. Heat shimmered around her fingers as a fiery eel burst to life.

The blood drained from Simon's face. Pickett grabbed her cloak, preparing to hurl it at him. The world seemed to slow and, for a gruesome moment, she wondered what it would be like to live in a world without Simon. Not with him gone but with him really, truly absent from the world.

It wasn't a world she wanted.

She had only just thrown off her outer cloak, ready to use the runes to shield him, when a pitcher flew through the air, smacking Corsa directly in the face.

Pottery smashed. Corsa screamed, then thumped to the ground, and Nancy panted, her lip curled. She opened her mouth, furrowed her brows and stammered, "You-you fucker!"

"Simon, we have to go now!" Pickett snapped.

"But I—"

"Back door, come on." Nancy grabbed both their hands and dragged them down the hall, letting go only to grab a torch from one of the wall sconces. Pickett threw one last look over her shoulder, just in time to see Corsa twitching. They didn't have much time.

"Wait!"

Pickett fumbled with her pockets, snatching up one of the jars of blackout powder. It wouldn't last too long but it might distract Corsa enough for them to make an escape. She hurled it at the ground, plunging the hall into darkness.

"What did you do that for?" Simon demanded. "Now we can't see!"

"I know the way," Nancy insisted. "Better than Corsa. I've apprenticed here on and off my whole life. Turn right and follow the torchlight."

They raced through the dark until they reached the edge of the dust's reach, nearly slamming into the alley door. Pickett kicked it open. Simon turned, his eyes bright with tears as he took Nancy's hands.

"Darling, listen to me. I don't know what deal that woman has with your father, but she's working for the Gilt King. I know because she was there when he hired me. She's a spy for your father's enemy. Whatever you do, don't trust her."

Oh fuck. Pickett glanced over her shoulder. This would have been a perfect time for Edie to magically show up with the solution to free Nancy. But she was nowhere in sight, of course not.

Nancy sucked in a sharp breath, her eyes going wide. "Then I'm not my father's hostage," she whispered.

"Darling, I fear this is much, much worse than we realized."

Pickett was torn between two minds. She could take Simon and run. That was the smart thing to do, at least. But Corsa was working for the Gilt King, and she'd been made, which put the poor girl in twice the danger. Pickett couldn't leave Nancy here. She couldn't take her out of the temple either.

Nancy set her jaw, her eyes going red and glossy.

"I am done with being everyone's puppet," she snarled, shoving the torch at Pickett.

"What are you . . .?" Pickett began, but she didn't have time to finish her thought.

Nancy rolled up the sleeve to reveal her runes, snatched the torch back, and pressed it to her skin.

"Nancy!" Simon shouted as Nancy screamed. The air reeked with burnt flesh. Pickett lunged forward, snatching back the torch, but it was done. Where once there had been runes, Nancy now had only a burned mess.

She whimpered, tears streaming down her face as she stumbled forward into the alleyway.

"You lunatic," Simon gasped, pulling her close. "You absolute madwoman."

Nancy just laughed wetly and held her arm to her chest.

"Get me out of here before Corsa catches up," she commanded.

It appeared they'd be able to make use of Lady Elowey's cart after all. Maybe some god or other was smiling on them because Simon hadn't given her time to call it off. This was actually going to work.

"This way," Pickett barked.

They raced down the alley, lit by the torch and the dying light of dusk, and skidded around the corner to the absence of a cart.

Just a horse and a servant with the Elowey crest stitched into his tunic. He stared at them. Pickett stared back. Then he pulled a folded letter from his pocket, dropped it on the ground, mounted the horse, and trotted off.

Pickett scrambled for the letter, ripping the paper as she opened it.

"What does it say?" Simon demanded.

Pickett's arms fell to her sides as she watched the retreating ass of the Elowey horse. The torch slipped from her fingers and fell to the ground, sputtering in the dirt for a moment before it died.

"It offers all the goodwill I earned," she muttered. "During my servitude in the Elowey household."

TWENTY-FOUR

Nancy clutched at Simon's shirt and let out a small gasp of pain. Her arm oozed blood amidst the dark char of her burned skin.

Fucking Simon and his fucking impulses. Fucking Corsa and Elowey and the whole fucking city of Southfen.

"We can't take her to the Spotted Dick," Simon insisted. "Come on. I know a place where we can regroup."

Simon led them through the streets, one arm supporting a hobbling Nancy, who panted and tucked her arm to her chest. It wasn't long before they left behind the stone and gravel for rougher, smaller buildings on dirt paths. Simon slipped in through the back of one of them, and Pickett followed him inside, to what appeared to be a somewhat shabby kitchen. No sooner had the door behind her closed than another one at the end of the room burst open, and in stomped a woman with wild gray hair and a fire poker.

"You fuckin' trespassin' lazy—"

She froze, glancing between them, brows furrowing. "Simon, you know our arrangement."

"I know," he muttered. "A tea service for an hour's safety. I'll even go for two for medical supplies." He shifted, squeezing Nancy a little closer. She let loose a little whimper, which was probably for the best. Because all it took was Simon adding in, "Anni. Please. I love her."

And there it was. She lowered the fire poker and huffed.

"Two tea services and a handsome tip." She nodded to her left. "Pine box has bandages. Wash it first so the girl doesn't lose her arm. Then I'm putting you at the crooked table."

"Always a pleasure, Anni."

Pickett dug through the box to find the bandages as he rinsed off the mess that was her arm. Nancy hissed and scraped her heels against the floor.

"Sorry," Simon muttered. "Sorry, sorry, it'll be better soon."

Nancy gritted her teeth and gave a terse nod.

"So you've been in Southfen enough to have regular haunts?" Pickett knelt on the ground next to them.

"I have connections all over," Simon said. "It's how I met Nancy."

"He was working for a shipping company that owed my father money," Nancy muttered, holding out her arm.

"And what a wild romance it's turned into," Pickett said dryly, wrapping the bandages tightly around Nancy's arm. To her credit, the girl held firm. Only the tears pricking at her eyes hinted to just how much pain she was in. "It'll leave a scar, but hopefully once I'm done it'll hurt a bit less."

Nancy sniffed and blinked, which only made one of the tears fall. Wordlessly, she reached for Simon, who wrapped her in his arms. She'd gone the kind of pale that someone did before they got sick.

"We need a new plan," Simon said before pressing a kiss to Nancy's head.

That was like saying the swamp stank. Pickett pushed herself to her feet. "We also need to get something in her before she starts to shake. Take us to this crooked table."

THE TEA ROOM itself wasn't anything special. A few fishermen slumped over their tables, sipping from mismatched cups as a lethargic lutist plucked glumly at their instrument. Clearly all the good establishments would be on the pleasure street they'd left behind. Hopefully that meant nobody here would find them interesting enough to listen to. But it also meant if Edie was simply late, she'd have no idea where to rendezvous.

The thought made Pickett's gut clench.

"Edie and Jodiah aren't back, and we can't safely communicate to them that the plan has changed."

"If they're still at the bar, we could send a messenger," Simon said.

"Bar?" Nancy asked softly.

"My bar, it's . . ." Pickett pinched the bridge of her nose. "Fuck. If Corsa's working for the Gilt King, she's probably already told him we broke Nancy out. Only now she knows we know, which we weren't supposed to know. The bar and brothel aren't safe places to go."

"I don't care about him. I only cared about getting Nancy out of there." Simon squeezed Nancy's hand, and she smiled and squeezed it back.

"We can pay a fishmonger and lie low for a few days," she insisted.

"Assuming the Gilt King doesn't own the fishmonger," Pickett said. "Nancy, this man owns half of Southfen. You're the daughter of his biggest rival. He paid Corsa to keep you trapped in the temple. He hired Simon to break you out."

Simon narrowed his eyes. "It is pretty bizarre when you put it that way."

"He's controlling every move and when it's made. Like a sheepdog herding us all into a pen. Simon here recognizing

Corsa has fucked those plans right up. He's going to be coming for all of us."

Anni trudged up with a tray, which she plopped down unceremoniously onto the table, half slinging their cups at them along with a teapot and a plate of scones that looked like maybe some of the flour had been cut with plaster. She then shoved a hand in Simon's direction.

"I believe you made me pay for two," he said. "So maybe a second pot. Maybe a fruity flavor. My companion here likes fruit."

Anni snorted but didn't move until Simon dropped a coin in her palm. How suave and gentlemanly could he continue to be once that money of his ran out?

Pickett nudged the plate of scones toward Nancy. "Eat. That wound on your arm's gonna give you shakes. If you don't eat, you'll be sick."

Nancy picked at the scone, only taking a few bites after a few tense moments of both Pickett and Simon staring at her.

"All this time I thought it was my father who had Corsa put the rune on me," she murmured.

"Is it better or worse to know it was just a prick taking advantage of star-crossed lovers?" Pickett asked.

"Dragon's teeth," Nancy muttered, then stuffed another bite of scone into her mouth.

"If it's any consolation, I suspected your father, too," Pickett said. Which did not feel great. In fact, it was a feeling uncomfortably close to what she might actually call "guilt." Which was absurd. Fistic was the richest man in Southfen. He'd been willing to take the bar from her if she couldn't meet his ridiculous repayment terms. He was, well, a father, it turned out. He'd probably hired Corsa because he thought a runecrafter could keep Nancy safe. Well, at least he thought he'd hired Corsa.

He was going to get off that boat and sleep peacefully in the finest house in town, convinced his daughter was safe. He had no idea Corsa had been bought out from under him or that Nancy was the Gilt King's pawn.

"Oh fuck," Pickett murmured. "I can't believe I'm going to say this, but I think we need to lay low tonight and go to Fistic in the morning. This time, both of you come with me. We tell him everything. We tell him about Corsa and that the Gilt King is probably waiting to snatch us all up as soon as he finds us to keep his leverage."

Nancy's eyes widened. "You can't be serious."

"You must have hit your head," Simon insisted.

"Fistic is still the most powerful person in Southfen," Pickett pointed out. "He'll be invested in remaining so. Look. Will he be angry? Yes."

"Definitely," Simon said.

"He might send me back to the temple," Nancy argued.

"Not if we tell him why you injured your arm," Pickett argued. "We come to him with evidence that this guy is fucking with his daughter? He might be so shocked Simon won't look like the worst fellow in the world anymore. And, more importantly, he can keep us protected. We don't know what the Gilt King will do with us, but we know your father wouldn't hurt you. If a war's about to start, I'd rather be on his side."

Simon and Nancy exchanged glances, then Nancy's brows furrowed.

"I-I don't like it," she said. "It's risky, but it's better than letting him go on trusting Corsa. That raises a bigger question. If the Gilt King had access to me all along, why did he bother with you and Simon? He could have had Corsa remove me from that temple whenever he liked."

Pickett opened her mouth then closed it.

"He suggested I find a witch," Simon said. "He specifically said I should bring on a witch to help me rescue you. Sonora is called the Swamp Witch."

"He's after us for some reason," Pickett muttered.

Her insides churned. The Spotted Dick, the bar, her brother, all of this was a whirlpool swirling around her. Had Edie been caught up in its current?

"All the more reason we need Fistic on our side now," Pickett said.

Simon and Nancy glanced at each other then back to Pickett.

"I suppose my father does need to know about Corsa," she said softly. "And if you can convince him to protect Simon, too, then we can send a messenger to the bar to see if the others are still there."

"Then let's go," Picket said, rising from the table. Simon kept one arm tight around Nancy as he helped her to her feet. She still clutched her bandaged arm to her chest. Maybe her looking pathetic could work in their favor. Marching up to the richest man in Southfen and declaring that she'd knowingly lied to him and that his employee was a traitor might not go well. And Edie wasn't back. That was a dangerous line of thinking because if she started ruminating . . .

Pickett opened the door to the tea shop and froze at the sight of a bound girl.

"Edie," she breathed.

TWENTY-FIVE

Of all the horrible scenarios she could have pictured, this wasn't one of them. Edie, her mouth gagged, hands bound in front of her, bag confiscated. There were other figures, too. Big, hulking brutes, but Pickett could barely register them. Her hand balled into a fist. Her feet moved and she tried to launch herself forward, but one of those blurry, inconvenient shapes caught her.

"Hold on!" Simon cried, and there was the click of a cocking crossbow.

"Let her go!" Pickett shouted, trying to claw at her assailant's face. And it was only then, pressed up against his chest, that she was the embroidered seal on his breast.

Her heart pounded. Her ears rang. No. No no no. This wasn't the plan.

"You keep that shrew contained," the man rumbled. "We were told it was preferential to bring you in unharmed but, well, needs must."

Pickett's vision widened just enough to see Jodiah behind Edie, a rope wrapped tightly around his whole torso, his left eye swollen. One of the brutes pointed Jodiah's crossbow at them just for good measure.

"Let her go," Simon said. "That lady's got no part of this. In fact, she's a total stranger. Never seen her before in our lives. Right? And also, whatever she did, we're not involved."

Even Nancy turned to stare at him, utterly baffled. Perhaps she was finally coming to terms with what a stonebrain she was choosing to marry.

"Afraid we can't," the brute rumbled. "We've caught word that this young woman confessed to a murder a few months back."

Pickett met Edie's tear-filled eyes and finally straightened.

"It was self-defense," Pickett insisted.

The man chuckled and caught Pickett's chin, forcing her to look into his gray eyes. "Oh yeah? Well half a dozen terrified villagers think she's a menace."

"And I know you're not fool enough to believe them." She swallowed, glancing back down onto that crest on his chest—a crown cut through with a sword. She'd never seen this particular design, but it didn't take a scholar to guess its owner. This guy was as subtle as an earthquake. "The Gilt King's establishing a Southfen police force now?"

The other two men chuckled. Edie balled her hands into fists. Without use of her arms, she couldn't do much more than that.

"In fact, she's our first arrest," another one said. "And you will be our second, caught red-handed kidnapping a young patroness from the temple of Al-Dagos."

Pickett glanced over her shoulder. Nancy grabbed Simon's shoulder, her hand trembling. Simon worked his jaw, glancing between the men before he met Pickett's eyes. She gave a small shake of her head.

"What are you going to do with us?" Nancy demanded.

"Afraid the Gilt King is a little put out with you lot. Dunno what you did but he's got plans." He grinned so wide his eyes crinkled at the edges. "You're coming with us."

Simon looked ready to throw a punch. Pickett could see how this would go. A brawl in the street followed by Simon on the ground with his neck snapped, and they would still end up with the Gilt King. But she still had a bottle of blackout powder. She considered throwing it on the ground right there, but it might only earn them a few seconds before the wind dispersed it. And the result would be the same—knives and crossbow bolts.

Pickett took a deep breath and slipped over to Jodiah's side, stuffing her hands in her pockets.

"Right then. Let's get where we're going before dark," she said. "I do hope the Gilt King has dinner for us."

CHAPTER

TWENTY-SIX

Of course they were being marched to the Elowey estate. Pickett didn't even try to hide her scowl as they were led inside. On the one hand, she was back with Edie. On the other, they were all being escorted under threat of stabbing.

Spidernose was nowhere to be seen as they were marched inside, though a few servants watched with wide eyes. Nobody tried to stop them. That was all Pickett needed to know—that they were entirely expected. She locked eyes with one and scuffed her heel against the floor, just for good measure.

Clearly, the Gilt King's hired brutes were familiar with the layout of the Elowey estate because they didn't hesitate in their movements. They knew exactly where to bring the five of them.

The room they were led to was nothing extravagant compared to the others in the estate: a bed, a chest of drawers, and a nice rug. And yet it had a grand view of Southfen in the distance. That was enough to set Pickett's skin prickling. Why would they be placed in a room with a view like that? Surely they should be stuffed in a closet or whatever the Eloweys had that equated to a dungeon.

"This way," the brutes grunted, dragging Jodiah and Simon back.

"Wait! Simon!" Nancy shouted, lurching toward them, but the brute shoved her back onto the bed.

"You stay here."

"Where are you taking them?" Pickett demanded, taking a step forward.

But the brute barred her path. "Their own accommodations. Don't worry. The boss ain't gonna hurt 'em."

He slammed the door behind him. Pickett swore and tried the handle, but it wouldn't budge. So that's why they were in this room. It locked from the outside. Pickett growled to herself before she rushed to Edie's side, ripping off the gag and pulling her into a tight hug.

"Where were you?" she demanded. "I was half out of my wits."

"I'm fine," Edie assured her, squeezing her back just as tightly.

A sudden whimper filled the room. Pickett reluctantly released Edie to find Nancy slumped against the bed, her hand pressed to her arm. The bandages and her face had both gone bright pink.

"F-fuck," Nancy whimpered. "This has all just gone so fucking wrong."

Pickett was about to move to Nancy's side but Edie beat her. She plopped down onto the bed and wrapped an arm around Nancy's shoulder.

"I'm sorry I didn't get back sooner," she said. "I was hoping to find a way to remove your runes, but I was held up. Obviously."

Nancy blinked, fresh tears streaming down her cheeks. "Who-who are you?"

"I'm Edie. I'm a friend of Pickett's. We-we were trying to

rescue you." They both glanced down at Nancy's arm, and Pickett cringed.

"I see you went the maiming route after all," Edie murmured.

"Don't blame me. It turns out Nancy here is even crazier than we are." This girl wanted freedom so badly she'd burned herself to be with her lover, and she was just as much a prisoner as if she hadn't done it.

Nancy sniffled again. "For all the good it did me. Still a prisoner."

"So what happened?" Pickett demanded, turning to Edie.

"Exactly what it looks like." Edie shook her head. "I'd barely stepped foot in Southfen before they grabbed me. They knew where I'd be, I'm sure of it. Said they were apprehending me for past crimes. Beat the tar out of Jodiah when he tried to fight. Then they kept us stuffed in a granary until a messenger came and told them where to find you."

"This guy's got eyes everywhere," Pickett muttered.

"Um." Nancy looked Edie up and down. "What did they mean by past crimes?"

"I killed a man in self defense a while back," Edie sighed, resting her chin on one hand. "But how could they have known?"

"You did announce that you were an assassin to an angry mob," Pickett pointed out.

"Yes, but I was lying."

"Yes, but they didn't know that."

Nancy blinked and scooted away from Edie.

For a girl willing to attack a sorceress and burn her own arm, Nancy Fistic was awfully squeamish. Pickett shook her head.

"More to the point, Edie, did you find a way to remove the runes safely?" she demanded. "I'd hate to think what'll happen if that runecrafter slaps another one on one of us."

"The runecrafter?" Edie furrowed her brows. "Hang on. We're the Gilt King's prisoners. Doesn't she work for Fistic?"

"Nope, the Gilt King bought the sorceress out from underneath him."

Edie pulled a face. "So we've pulled her out of the fire—"

"And tossed her into a slightly different-colored fire, yeah." Pickett sighed.

"And a foul smelling one to boot," Edie said. "The runes can only be safely removed by the caster. I can use my trick to move it around, but I can't get rid of it without . . ." She wrinkled her nose and gestured at Nancy's arm.

"We're so fucked." Nancy's voice came out a little weaker than before. She wrapped her arms around her middle and stared at the floor. Her eyes began to glisten with unshed tears. "I just wanted to get married. I didn't want to ruin my father's business or get anybody hurt."

Pickett hesitated then nudged Nancy's shoulder. "There are probably ways this could be worse. I mean, we're being held hostage, sure, but it's a cushy room. You got to smash lips with Simon again, which I guess you find fun. And it's probably in the Gilt King's best interest to keep both you and your father alive, too. So everything's going to work out just—"

A distant boom cut her off. Nancy screamed and jumped up so suddenly she smashed into the bedside table, knocking an expensive-looking vase to the ground. Edie's hands flew to her mouth. Pickett turned slowly toward the window to find pieces of buildings falling down to the ground on the skyline of Southfen. The finest of them, Fistic's house, burned. Tiny spots she could only assume were his many birds raced out through the windows as servants stumbled out the doors. Gods' balls. How many of them were dead?

"No," Nancy whispered, her voice barely audible. "My father. What if-if he was home?" She wrapped her arms around her middle as her whole body began to tremble and sway. After a moment, her knees gave and she sank to the ground. That poor girl was going to run out of tears soon.

The door opened. One of the Gilt King's men stepped in. "Our master would like a word with the witch."

"Fuck off," Edie snarled, jumping to her feet, but Pickett caught her arm.

"We're not in a position to do anything," she whispered.

Edie grasped the hem of Pickett's runed cape. "You can't go without me."

"I'd rather you were here to keep her safe." Pickett nodded toward the Nancy puddle on the floor and forced herself to smile. "I'll be back before you realize I'm gone. You know me."

That didn't seem to be the right thing to say, though, because Edie's cheeks flushed and she looked ready to cry. Pickett took a deep breath and forced herself to turn away, following the man out of the room. He locked it behind her, and Pickett had a sudden, impulsive urge to knee him in the groin, bust through the door and . . . And what?

"This way," he grunted before leading her down the hall and to the library.

Fantastic. It looked like another delightful meeting with Lady Elowey. Pickett sighed and stepped into the room. But it wasn't Elowey who sat on the settee.

Pickett's heart pounded. Her mouth went dry. How many years had she wanted to see him again? How many years had she decided he was dead? That he'd abandoned her? That his role in her life was over? There was a little gray in his hair. She hadn't been there to see it sprout. She'd have teased him for graying young. And a scar marred his brow that hadn't been there before.

He broke into a wide smile as he rose, holding out his hands like he was about to dance with her.

"Pickett."

"Patr."
Fucking perfect.

TWENTY-SEVEN

Patr's name bounced around in her skull like a trapped beetle.

Patr. Patr. Patr.

Patr who'd held her and wanted her. Patr who'd led her into Coldspine. Patr who'd left her.

He took a step toward her.

She took a step back.

His smile faltered, but at least he had the good sense to lower his arms. "Pickett, I know this must be complicated for you."

"Well, I've spent a few years, thinking you were dead." Pickett straightened and balled her hands into fists. "Grief does wonders for clear thinking."

Patr's brows twitched. He shifted, but he didn't take another step forward. "I thought you knew. I sent the letter to Merca two years ago."

Pickett let out a wry laugh and flexed her fingers. "Haven't been back in a while."

"But surely you recognized me." He shifted toward her, his

lips twitching into a not-quite smile. "I know you saw her recently, so you must have guessed. I mean, Gilt King? Bresk?"

"The fuck are those supposed to mean to me?"

This time, Patr's expression fully shifted into one of shock. He stepped forward as Pickett stepped back, and she snatched the first book off the shelf she could reach, brandishing it like a club. Edie would keel over if she could see.

Patr stopped, eyes widening. He held up his hands. "Pickett. Darling. Gilt King. The tavern where I left you was the Gilded Son. Bresk? That was the name of the priest who married us. Your friend told you that name at least, yes?"

Pickett almost dropped the book. "Are you serious? Why the fuck would I remember any of those things?"

"Because they were our past!" Patr shouted.

Pickett tightened her grip on the book. It would be so easy to hurl it at his head. But it was Patr. After years apart, it was still Patr.

She clenched her jaw and flung the book across the room.

"What the fuck is going on?" she demanded.

"Darling, I know you're upset, but please, have a seat."

"Patr, so help me if you call me that again, I'll blacken your eye."

Patr heaved a sigh but sank down onto the settee, Picketless.

"Whether or not you read it, I wrote you a letter of apology. In Coldspine I had some bad luck with the mercenaries I was sent to barter with, but a new opportunity arose. There was no time to go back for you and nobody would spare a messenger for free. And I was down to my last coin."

So he could have sent word and he chose not to. He complained of being down to his last coin, but she'd had nothing. It had taken a year to numbly work and barter and hitch her way back down south to the place that felt most like home, before it hit her that she'd abandoned the Dames in the middle of the night. She had no home. She'd given it up for him, and he couldn't spare one coin to send word.

Her cheeks burned, but she bit the inside of her cheek before that burn could spread to her eyes. She wouldn't cry, not in front of him. She wouldn't give him the satisfaction.

"It seems to have worked out well for you," Pickett grumbled.

"Yes. I became quite a competent runecaster. I learned how to invest in businesses and reap the benefits. And once I thought I was in a position to give you the life you deserved"—he offered her a shy smile—"I came back for you. I'm going to give you the life I always promised."

"Yeah. Well." Pickett sniffed and crossed her arms. "You didn't come back soon enough."

Patr's expression flickered, but he nodded. "I know. But I'm here now. And look at the good I've done." He began counting off on his fingers. "I fixed up the Spotted Dick. I'm in the process of establishing a security force to provide a little order around here. I invested in your bar, did the repairs."

"It was fine before."

"The rotting floorboards say otherwise." He smiled wryly at her. "I even educated your girl. I gave her all the runic sequences she needed to learn so she could protect you, or are we pretending I had nothing to do with that runed cape?"

Picket clutched the hem of her cape. "Are you fucking kidding me?"

"I couldn't very well approach you," he insisted. "But I wanted to make sure you were safe. As soon as I found out where you were, I just wanted to come to you." He shifted, moving to stand, but a sharp look from Pickett kept him seated. "But obviously the time wasn't right. So I did everything I could and look!" He beamed and gestured to the library at large. "You can have your revenge. Throw another book. Throw a whole shelf." He grabbed one of the settee pillows and hurled it across the room. "Lady Elowey looks down on the likes of us, but she's in my pocket. She denies you a cart? I'll make her home my stronghold and give it to you. You can't imagine how good it feels, Pickett, to have, to finally get what we've wanted for so long."

What she wanted? Pickett couldn't ever recall saying she wanted any of this. Then her brain caught up.

"Wait. How did you know she denied me a cart?"

Patr had the decency to look a little sheepish. "After your meeting with her, I asked what it was about."

"And how did you know I'd gone to see her?" she asked. "And the tea house. I know you've got eyes everywhere, but you seem to suddenly know everywhere I am given Simon had to tell you about the bar."

Patr didn't respond. Shocking for someone who couldn't shut his mouth a minute ago. So the explanation was a bad one. She glanced down at herself, and those runes on her cape caught her eye. Slowly, she shrugged it off and held it up.

"Does every rune in that pamphlet do what it says it does?" she asked.

Patr glanced away and shook his head. It was like a slap to the face.

Pickett screamed and hurled the cape at him. Patr caught it, jumping to his feet.

"You used her!" she snapped. "You meddled in our lives and endangered us! You tricked her into tracking me, didn't you?"

"It was just something to inform me of your whereabouts. It's not harmful. I designed it myself."

"And what about the rune on Nancy's arm?" Pickett snapped. "Is that another creation of yours?"

Patr went very still. His expression hardened into something cold and unreadable. Something that didn't suit him at all. He folded the cape and set it on the settee before folding his hands behind his back.

"Her father is the very sort of man who used to look down on us."

"He's a bit of an ass, but he's not evil."

Patr let out a bark of laughter. "Isn't he? Darling, he sold you into servitude to pay off your debt. He's the one who hired me on that fool's errand in Coldspine. Oh, you can be sure Hurb Fistic got his money, but I lost you."

Pickett sucked in a sharp breath then let it out. "You're the one who chose to push on to the next job without me."

"I was desperate. I had to! Why pity that moneylender? He's been the richest man in Southfen for years and what has he done with it?" He stalked to the window and jerked it open. The smell of the sea brine and distant smoke filled the library.

Patr jabbed his hand out into the open air. "Look out at it, Pickett. It's a mess of shanty buildings without any central authority. I mean, can you even say who the current Ward King is? No. Because nobody gives a shit because nobody's tried to turn it into something better." He moved toward her, gesturing this way and that, his eyes shining. "I have the resources now. Finally, a gutter rat of Southfen can turn it into one of the great cities of the continent."

Pickett took another step back until the wall pressed against her shoulders. Patr stopped only an arm's length away.

"Please," he pleaded. "Do this with me. Your girl can run the bar. You can live in leisure here with me. The tolls from the new road alone will set us up like royals."

She reached for the nearest thing she could find and landed on a dull knife. A letter opener. If she jammed it forward, she could take out an eye. She could at least hurt him bad enough to slow him down if it came to it.

The thought of doing that, though, made her eyes sting.

"You always had big dreams," she whispered. "But this is too much. Using Edie and my brother. Tracking me. The runes on Nancy's arm. You know she had to burn it off, right? And then you blow up her father's house." She swallowed. "It's not a good way to start off a career as Southfen's benevolent ruler."

"It's a hard world, darling. We both know that. And the power of a reputation." He brushed his fingers against her cheek, and Pickett flinched. It would be so easy to stab him with the letter opener, to knee him in the groin, even to slap him. But it was Patr.

Patr who was alive.

Patr who was her husband.

The tears began to blur her vision. She clenched her jaw, willing them not to fall. "I don't want this," she bit out. "You're hurting people."

"But I'd never hurt you. Wife."

He cupped her cheek with his hand, then let it slide to the back of her neck and something stung, sharp and quick as a wasp. Pickett gasped, slapping his hand away, but she was already pressed up against the wall. There was nowhere else to go. She dropped the letter opener and pressed her hand to her neck. The skin at the base of her skull was raised like old scar tissue. She knew the pattern Nancy had burned off her own arm.

"You bastard!" she shrieked, hurling herself at him. Patr sidestepped, grabbing her to pull her into a tight hug.

"I know," he whispered. "I know it's cruel. But I'm going to keep you safe. I can cast this rune at a time, and I'm choosing you."

"To trap me," she gasped.

"To keep you close so I can protect you, darling, so stop fighting."

The rune on her neck stung and, for the life of her, Pickett couldn't bring herself to give him the pummeling he so rightly deserved.

He smiled sadly down at her. "When I'm done, you'll be a princess. But today, I'll keep you safe."

He pressed a kiss to her forehead. Pickett squeezed her eyes shut, a few fat tears finally escaping.

She'd been wrong. The Patr she knew was dead.

TWENTY-EIGHT

She was taken to a different room, separate from the others. It must have been one Patr had taken for himself. There was a trunk full of papers, another set of boots, a traveling cloak that would fit him. It should have felt familiar. How many nights had she spent in an inn or a rented room where she'd seen his things scattered around?

Pickett sank down onto the ground next to the trunk and started grabbing at the papers. Full of contracts, deeds, and sketches of runes, it was a box of power for him. She read through them one by one, desperate for some sign that this wasn't him. Someone else had pushed him to do it. A demon or something had taken hold of him. But no, it was all him.

He'd bought up the whole village of Gristlark, and now its poor flocked to Southfen, searching for work in places like the Spotted Dick. That explained the beggars and new fruit stands. Wealth had to come from somewhere. He'd imported a cart of black powder weeks before. No doubt, it was what he'd used to destroy Fistic's house. He'd studied and designed his own runes.

Pickett pressed her fingers to her neck, feeling his mark. Had he always been like this? She could wring out every memory of him, question every word he ever spoke to her, and yet the signs weren't there.

No, they were. She just couldn't remember them, for the same reason she couldn't jab the letter opener into his eye—the same reason she'd left with him.

Perhaps she could cut the mark away, like they had for Nancy. Experimentally, she tried digging her nails into the skin, but it was like clawing at stone. Whatever this mark was, he was clearly not going to let Pickett go nearly as easily as Nancy.

Pickett squeezed her eyes shut. A lump formed in her throat, but no fresh tears came to her eyes. She must have cried them all out already.

Numbly, she began undoing her braids on the left side. The tight curls bounced free, lovelier than they'd been before Merca got her hands on them. If things had worked out the way they were supposed to, maybe she'd have taken the woman's advice, started tending to herself a little more with rouge and oils and charms. She'd have made herself pretty for a future with Edie.

A key clicked in the lock on the door. Pickett pulled the freed curls down, hiding the mark as she scrambled to her feet. The door opened and in stepped Lady Elowey, looking like someone had swapped her perfume for horse piss. She had a couple of gowns draped over one arm. Servant work. It looked like she was finally forced to question just how worthwhile it truly was to work with the Gilt King.

"My darling." Patr swooped in past her, reaching for Pickett's hands.

She jerked back. His expression flickered before settling into something more neutral.

"We have time," he said with a little smile before gesturing to the door. "Lady Elowey has some dresses for you and your friend to change into. Nothing fancy, but I assure you she has no further need of them."

Elowey didn't move. Patr cleared his throat. When she remained still, he nudged her in the ribs. She curled her lip and without even glancing at Pickett, lay both out on the bed.

Patr inclined his head. "Now that's settled. I'm about to become the most powerful man in Southfen. It's going to call for a party. I'll send Edie in to help you get ready."

He winked at her, then waved a hand at the door. "Lady Elowey, you may leave us."

Elowey paled, no doubt appalled to be dismissed like a servant, but shot Pickett one final sneer before slipping out.

A moment later, the door flew open and Edie threw herself at Pickett, wrapping her arms tightly around her shoulders. Pickett wanted to hug her back. She wanted to squeeze her close and never let go, but Patr was still there watching her every move like a cat on the prowl. Her gut churned. When this night was over, she was going to ensure that Edie made it back home.

"I'll see the both of you soon," Patr said when he got enough of what he wanted to see from them. "Enjoy the gowns, ladies."

He offered Pickett that soft, self-assured smile that had once convinced her to cross a continent with him before he slipped out the door.

"Edie." Pickett pulled back, cupping Edie's face. She looked all right. Good. She could keep it that way for a few hours. "How is Nancy?"

"There's a healer in with her right now," Edie said, gripping Pickett's hands. "Her arm's getting patched up. They didn't let me see the boys. Pickett, I'm so sorry. If I'd gotten back sooner, I know I could have done something about—"

"The rune," Pickett bit, and she could feel her cheeks warming. "You said you can maybe move it. If-if they put one of those on us, could you move it to, I dunno, a pot or a wall? Something else?" She swallowed. "You know, just planning ahead."

Edie shook her head. "At best I could move it from flesh to flesh. I'm sorry."

That settled it. Pickett was trapped. She was just a turtle caught in a trap, destined for somebody's soup. Patr knew exactly what he was doing. He'd figured out where she was, how to draw her out, and how to keep her in his web. He was always going to find a way to lead her right here.

"It's fine." Pickett swallowed and turned to the contracts, digging through them. "He left files in here. He must have wanted me to see them. Maybe something could be useful for Fistic to fight Patr with?"

Edie shook her head. "Fistic is probably dead after what happened with his house. The Gilt King was now the dominant power in Southfen. What could any of these documents possibly do to stop him?"

Pickett let some of the papers slide from her hands and back onto the floor. He could drive another village into the ground. He could build his road and boost his profits, drown her bar and Southfen, and still never miss a meal. She sank down to the ground.

"Edie, I don't know what to do. I can't fool him into thinking I'm a witch. He knows me. And he's taken over everything."

Edie sat down next to her, staring at the papers before she finally said, "He called you darling."

Pickett swallowed thickly. Once she said it, it would be out there. She couldn't take it back. But maybe it was time. After all, what had secrets ever given her but trouble? She could hide the rune to spare Edie knowing a little longer, but this? There was no point. "He's my husband."

Edie's expression didn't change, but her fingers twitched into a half-fist. "You said once someone hurt you. It was him, wasn't it?"

Pickett sighed and gestured to the papers. "He left me to pursue all of this. I left the Spotted Dick to be with him. In Coldspine, he went off for work and never came back. I thought he was dead, so I left. I borrowed money and opened the Pick's

Pocket while he became the Gilt King. It looks like he's decided he wants me back. He's clearly doing whatever it takes to keep me in his net."

Edie squeezed her eyes shut, took a deep breath, then opened them as she let it out. She ran her hands over the papers, then plucked them up one at a time.

"What are these?"

"Contracts and deeds and other sorts of business stuff, mostly from Gristlark."

"Gristlark?"

Pickett sagged a little. "Some village. He bought up everything. Took the profits. Everyone he didn't own was put out of work. I have a feeling it's a strategy he'll use on every town the new road passes."

"So the bar."

"The only thing that'll keep us open is if he deigns to drive business our way. And even if he does, there'll be a lot of villagers who won't be able to afford half a beer. We'll be fucked. They'll be eviscerated."

"Fuck!" Edie ran a hand over her face. "Pickett, I'm so sorry. I should never have taken his money. I just thought . . . I don't know what I thought. It all seems ridiculous in hindsight."

"You trusted someone. That's all." She reached for Edie's hand. Edie gave it, twining their fingers together. It felt good. Like a mooring line in choppy seas. The world could go up in flames but Edie was still alive. She was still here.

"What do we do?" Edie asked.

"That depends." Pickett sat up a little straighter. "You said Nancy's all right?"

Edie shrugged. "Physically, yes. But she's traded one prison for another and, for all she knows, her father is dead."

Pickett forced herself to let go of Edie's hand so she could rise, hands on her hips. "We need to look for opportunity to get out of here. For now, though, we get dressed and go to dinner."

CHAPTER

TWENTY-NINE

The gowns sort of fit. Pickett's draped around her like a sack until she secured a braided belt around the middle. Edie's clung strangely to her bust and hips. But the silk was so soft it felt like water on her skin that wouldn't roll away. It would have been a luxury if it didn't feel like she was a horse being bridled for show.

Spidernose arrived, refusing to look directly at or speak to either of them. He simply wrinkled his spidery nose and jerked his head down the hall in a silent instruction for them to follow. Clearly, he was as fond of Patr setting up here as Lady Elowey.

He led them to the parlor this time, pausing only to shoot Pickett a parting sneer before retreating back down the hall. Pickett returned it with a gesture of her own before heading inside.

Patr sat in the largest of the cushioned chairs, a glass of wine in hand and Lady Elowey standing at his side, the comb back in her hair. Not that it distracted from the frown so deep it almost went down to her jaw. Across from him and separated only by a low, wooden table laden with ink, quill, and paper, sat Nancy. She also appeared freshly changed and, thank fuck, had visibly

180

clean bandages covering her arm. Corsa stood behind her, straight-backed and just a little smug, albeit with visible black powder stains on her skirt. In the other chair, looking a little waterlogged and significantly less coiffed than was his norm, sat none other than Hurb Fistic. Because of course he was here. Because of course he survived. He actually listened to Pickett, boarded a ship, and survived the destruction of his home and headquarters. All this time hoping to evade the rivalry between Fistic and the Gilt King, all this time hoping to help Nancy escape her father, and here they were, all of them gathered in the parlor.

Pickett couldn't help it. She didn't even try to. She braced herself on Edie's shoulder and began to giggle.

Fistic's eyes widened. For the first time since she'd known him, Pickett could spy no hunger—only rage.

"Traitor," he hissed. "You venomous hag! You set me up!"

"Don't talk that way about my sister!"

"Oh, Simon, you're here?" Pickett scrubbed a hand over her face and turned, surveying the room. At first, it was hard to pick Simon out. In his street clothes, he more or less blended in with the browns of the bookcases, though the dirt on his trousers certainly made him stand out. Simon was the only person bound to his chair. Even Jodiah, in a seat next to him, was free to move, not that he did. He sort of slumped in his seat, mouth half-open as he glanced sluggishly around the room.

Lady Elowey scoffed and flicked her wrist in Simon's direction. In a blink, Spidernose rushed behind him, whipping out a cloth to gag him. Jodiah lolled his head to the side to watch.

"What's wrong with him?" Pickett asked, jerking her thumb at the bounty hunter.

Jodiah raised his chin and bobbed his mouth as he focused his unswollen eye on her. That only lasted a second before he let his chin drop again.

"Laudanum," Spidernose said primly. "I'd say he's halfway to the Untamed Paradise right now."

"We like our guests comfortable and unclawed," Elowey said, drumming her fingers on her armrest.

"Comfortable," Fistic snorted.

Patr turned to him, his expression icy.

"You are far more comfortable now than you deserve," Patr said, swirling the wine in his cup. "But fortunately for myself and my friends, I am now the one who decides who gets what. And Sonora Pickett deserves ten times more than you could ever hope to accumulate."

So long as she stayed with him. From her position, she looked every bit to Fistic like a woman who'd set everything up to take him down, that she'd been on the Gilt King's side from the start. Pickett sobered a bit and hesitated. Was it better to let Fistic keep believing that? Was it better to come up with a lie to try and redirect Patr? What would actually help her get Nancy and Edie out of here?

Edie glanced at Pickett with a frown but said nothing. Until they had a plan, silence was the best option for them. It felt like wearing the wrong shoes.

"Vengeance never seemed your way," Fistic said, his lip curling as he looked her up and down in a way that made Pickett feel like beetle dung. Since when did she care what Fistic thought of her? But if she defended herself, it would mean taking a definite side.

Patr, on the other hand, beamed widely. "Vengeance? Maybe not. But I guarantee she can benefit a great deal more from her partnership with me." He gestured at Elowey and, without looking up, positively purred. "My good Lady Elowey, would you be so kind as to tuck that comb into my wife's hair?"

Elowey looked ready to keel over at the request. She whirled on Patr.

"My estate," she hissed. "My gowns—"

"Your holdings?" Patr gestured at the comb. "Is an ornament really worth sacrificing the profits you make from our partnership?"

"Partnership," she spat. The two of them glared each other down until, at last, she plucked the comb from her hair with two fingers as if it was a scorpion and held it out.

Patr leaned forward in his seat, his smug smile fading just a little. "I said to tuck it into her hair."

Pickett stiffened. Elowey stared at him. How much more could an ego take? For all she could tell, the woman was going to stab her with it. But at last, Elowey stepped forward, clumsily pressing it into the half-braided side of Pickett's hair. Pickett had to squeeze her hands together to stop herself from ripping it out and flinging it across the room.

Patr smiled again then gestured to the low table between them. "Now that we have the mood just right, I think it's time for business. Mr. Fistic, if you would be so kind, I've prepared a contract for you, already gave it my signature and all. Upon signing it, you will be granted a property in Gristlark where you can live out your life. A gesture of good will."

Fistic scowled and picked up the contract, almost immediately scoffing and dropping it. "In return for the entirety of my holdings in Southfen," he growled.

Patr shrugged. "With the new road underway, it's best it remains under a primary vision. Which means one person controlling all the investors."

"As well as all of my other investments." Fistic curled his lips. "You want to turn yourself into some sort of emperor."

"An empire needs its support, after all." Patr chuckled and drained the last of his glass. "You could refuse. Lady Elowey, your healer can provide more bandages, can't he?"

Corsa rested a hand on Nancy's head. The poor girl worked

her jaw as she stared down at her shoes. Simon grunted through his gag. The blood drained from Fistic's face. Well that was good as solved it. Pickett needed Patr to think she was properly cowed —or at least to lack the ideas as to how she might push back. She forced herself to let go of Edie's hand, even if it left her feeling like an unmoored buoy, and staggered over to Patr's side. Edie watched her go, eyes wide as a baby fawn's for just a moment before she moved to stand protectively next to Nancy.

Pickett rested a hand on Patr's shoulder, and he glanced up, eyes wide.

"Pickett?"

"Please." She swallowed and forced a smile. "I think an additional promise would be of use." She glanced at Nancy or, more specifically, Nancy's arm. "If he signs your contract, you must promise that neither you nor any machination of yours would harm her."

He furrowed his brows. "You think I would do that?"

"No," she lied, "but it would be a shame to start your empire on fear, wouldn't it? I thought you were going to turn Southfen into something great."

He searched her face, but Pickett had plenty of experience in hiding her feelings.

"Corsa?" Patr said. "In your experience with these two, will they behave themselves?"

Corsa met his gaze and gave a sharp, jerky nod.

It must have been what he needed because he finally nodded and rested his hand on Pickett's.

"Very well," he said. "I give you my word, Mr. Fistic. Once you sign it, you two will live long and naturally as guests in the estate I assign. I'll even provide protection, if that would please my wife." He raised his brows at Pickett.

She nodded in return. "Yes, it would."

Patr smiled again, but it was different than his smug smirk

from before. It was soft, open, heartbreaking. Pickett couldn't bear it, so she forced herself to turn back to Fistic.

"It's the wisest option open," she said softly, then inclined her head. "My friend."

Fistic frowned, but the wrathful spark had left his eyes. He picked up the quill, dipped it in the inkpot, and scribbled his name across the bottom of the document.

CHAPTER

THIRTY

The silence in the room was electric. Fistic's hand shook. For a moment, it looked as though he might spill the bottle of ink over the contract. A quick glance at Nancy, however, stilled him. With a heavy sigh, he set the quill down. It was done. War averted and blood unspilled, Patr had made himself the most powerful person in Southfen.

Gods help them all.

"Corsa," Patr said. "Now that this is done, I'd like for you to tend to the accommodations we discussed."

"Already? Are you sure you don't want me to . . ." Corsa gestured to Hurb and Nancy Fistic.

Patr shook his head. "I have things quite in hand here."

"Very well." Corsa ducked into a quick curtsy and swept out of the room. On the way out, she made a point of smacking into Pickett's shoulder

As soon as she left, Edie inched closer to the Fistics, kneeling down to look at the contract. Pickett had no idea what Edie's intentions were, but she could buy her some time.

Pickett cleared her throat and gestured to the room at large.

"Lady Elowey, my husband implied that you have a feast prepared?"

"Yes," Lady Elowey choked out, then flicked her wrist. "Hidge. Tend to it."

Spidernose bowed and swept out of the room, making sure to toss Pickett his perfunctory sneer on the way.

Pickett kept her back to him and smiled at Patr. He smiled back, though his expression stiffened.

"Darling, what are you thinking?"

Out of the corner of her eye, Pickett spied Edie running her finger down the page, her lips moving wordlessly with the text of the contract.

"I'm thinking that after all this trouble, Simon and Nancy might as well have a wedding dinner," Pickett said.

Patr arched a brow. "Darling?"

Pickett had to stop herself from smiling too sweetly at him. No sense in making him suspicious, after all.

"Patr," she said tartly, turning to face him, just so she could catch sight of Edie doing whatever the fuck she was doing over his shoulder. Whatever it was, Fistic seemed to approve at least. Pickett forced herself to look away from them and into Patr's eyes. "All of this has happened because Simon and Nancy wanted to marry. So here we are. The bride is here. The groom is here and unable to muck things up with his mouth. With my authority as a witch I can speak for the gods themselves and bless the union."

Jodiah moaned behind her.

Pickett turned and held up a hand. "Please, Jodiah, don't insult me in front of my husband. He won't care for it. I assure you, the gods won't mind."

Jodiah grunted, and a dribble of drool slid from his lower lip. Hard to tell if that meant he did or didn't understand what was going on. Pickett shrugged and returned her attention to Patr.

"Well? What do you say?"

Patr blinked, then grinned and nodded. "If that would make you happy, then I suppose additional celebration is in order."

He turned to the others, and Pickett caught her breath, but Edie had finished whatever she was doing and stood behind Nancy's chair, looking perfectly serene.

"Business first. Then merriment. One cannot celebrate a wedding that has not occurred, after all."

Patr clapped his hands together and nodded. "Excellent. Now, Nancy, come greet your soon-to-be husband."

She glanced to her father then Edie, before rising and shuffling away from the chair. As soon as she passed the low table, however, she picked up the pace and raced to Simon's side. Ah, nothing like untying and ungagging your lover before being bound together forever. As soon as Simon was free, he leaped to his feet and hugged her close, running his fingers through her dark hair.

For just a moment, the sting of memory pierced right through her. Pickett remembered that first night after she'd left the Spotted Dick. Patr and she had stopped in a small village, she couldn't recall the name of, but she'd never forget the small, wooden temple. She remembered the priest who looked as though he'd crawled out of the grave to perform the wedding. Bresk, apparently, was his name as Patr reminded her. Pickett's memory had her holding Patr's hands, her heart warm and full with the certainty that this was about to be the best part of her life. Was it possible to feel that and remember all the other details at the same time?

Pickett cleared her throat and stepped forward, raising her arms. "Right. So. It's pretty clear you two have been eager to get married. Let's get it over with. Patr. Jodiah. Edie. Elowey. Fistic. Do you five witness the union between these two?"

"Yes," Patr and Edie said without a moment's hesitation.

"Fine," Fistic muttered while Lady Elowey just grunted.

Jodiah moaned and drooled.

"All right. Well. Four is good enough. Simon, do you want to marry Nancy?"

"O-Of course," he stammered.

"Even though her father doesn't like you and just lost his empire?"

"I mean, yes?"

"Good." Pickett smiled at Nancy. "And, Nancy, do you want to marry Simon?"

"More than anything."

"Even though he's a fool who lost his ship and hired me of all people to liberate you?"

Nancy twined her fingers in his and smiled at him. "I don't care about any of that."

It was a little sappy, but Nancy had been through a lot. Pickett could forgive her that much. What she couldn't forgive was the way Patr stared at her, his smile warm. His hand twitched, as if he was very seriously considering taking hers. The thought made her stomach tighten in the worst way. Time to end this.

"Very well, then. I'll assume this means you two will honor and love and swear loyalty and whatnot to each other, so let's declare it done and get to dinner."

Simon hesitated. "Sonora, aren't we supposed to exchange tokens?"

"Oh. Right." Pickett patted herself down, but all she had was the comb. Fine. She didn't really want it anyway. With Lady Elowey looking on in horror, Pickett handed it to Simon, who smiled as he tucked it onto Nancy's hair. She smiled up at him, then hesitated before glancing back at Fistic.

"Father?"

With a sigh, Fistic tugged one of the rings off his finger and handed it to her. She tried to slip it onto Simon's ring finger, then his middle, before finally settling on his thumb. He beamed at her before sweeping her up into a passionate kiss.

Patr laughed and clapped. "Wonderful! And rest assured, you shall have a glorious honeymoon with the freedom to roam this fine estate."

Lady Elowey looked ready to choke. Simon and Nancy looked like they'd completely forgotten the severity of the situation. Awkwardly, Edie began to clap alongside Patr.

"Congratulations to the happy pair." Pickett pulled Simon into a tight hug. He gasped in surprise, either from the gesture or the sudden weight he probably felt in his pocket as Pickett transferred the blackout bottle to him.

When she pulled away, he blinked, his hand going to the bottle, then set his jaw. Good. At least he knew what he had to work with now. Pickett made a point to turn and hug Nancy, too, just to ensure she didn't look too biased in Simon's favor.

"Be sure to follow your heart," she said. "Wherever he goes."

Nancy nodded against her and hugged her back.

"Well, that's that," Pickett declared as she pulled away. "Now. Let's eat!"

THIRTY-ONE

Fistic, looking a little green after the proceedings, was sent off to his "chambers." Given the little smirk Patr wore when he said it, Pickett could only assume he wasn't being kept in the lap of luxury. That gave her some idea, at least, about where he was. Not that she could follow him. She had to follow behind her husband, into the dining hall she'd never been allowed to enter, and eat like this was a real wedding feast.

Patr pulled her seat out for her, which was awfully gallant of him given the fact that he could have forced Elowey to do it instead. The lady herself, along with the rest of the dinner party, had to pull out their own chairs. Well, everyone except Jodiah. He managed to stumble down the halls, half-supported by Simon, but twice he tried to walk right into the table. It took both halves of the newly married couple to get him into a chair.

Once everyone was settled, Patr beamed and held out a hand. Instantly, a servant materialized to set a goblet in it, soon followed by a whole team, placing drinks in front of the rest of them. Jodiah gulped his down with gusto.

"A toast!" Patr raised his goblet. "To the happy couple and a new age in Southfen."

Pickett and the rest of them somewhat sullenly sipped at the wine. It had all the punch of summer fruit without the burn of the cheap stuff. Fuck. It was the best wine Picket had ever had. She did not need to be enjoying herself at a time like this.

Pickett threw back the last of her wine and forced a smile as the food came out.

Grilled fish and vegetables. Roasted quail, eggs, and potatoes. Fresh bread so warm she could feel its heat if she dangled her hand over it, along with equally fresh butter. And that didn't even approach the absolute display of cakes scattered across the table. And yes, they had quite a lot going on at the moment, but Pickett couldn't resist picking up one of the little cakes.

From across the table, Elowey shot her a filthy look. "It's poor manners to begin with the sweets."

Pickett took a bite out of it and froze. It was like eating a cloud. "Fuck! That's delicious." She wolfed down the rest of it before wiping her fingers on the linen napkin. "If you'd bothered to send the cart, your fine estate might not have been chosen by my husband and you wouldn't have to watch my poor manners."

Edie's eyes widened and she gave a little shake of her head, but Pickett pushed forward. "I do hope Nancy's new comb was worth it."

"Trash," Elowey hissed.

Patr slammed his fist down on the table so hard their goblets toppled over, splashing wine across the fine tablecloth. Elowey blanched and hunched her shoulders as Patr towered over her.

"How dare you!" he shouted. "If you ever speak that way to my wife again, I will dissolve your every holding and turn you out onto the streets. You will beg for coins, and I will command that nobody spare you a single shim!"

Pickett glanced at the others, who looked similarly cowed by the tirade. Jodiah blinked sluggishly and sat up a little straighter. He must have been coming out of his stupor because he managed to mouth, "What the fuck?" Simon rested his hand on Nancy's. Pickett caught his eye and glanced from him to Nancy to Jodiah then back. Simon frowned, then raised his brows and patted the pocket with her little wedding gift in it. Thank fucks and every god who ever did. If ever there was a time for him to be clever, it needed to be now.

Pickett let out a wail, burying her face in her hands as she shook her shoulders. If she squeezed her eyes hard enough, she could just wring out a couple of tears.

Patr pivoted immediately, resting a hand on her shoulder. "My darling."

"It's been a long day," she said softly, folding her hands in her lap. "Please. I think I just need to retire early."

"Of course." He slipped his hand under her hair and brushed her neck. Or, at least, the rune still burned into her neck. "I've set out a nightgown for you. You should rest. I'll join you soon."

"I'll go, too," Edie cut in. "Someone needs to help her out of that gown."

"Perhaps I should also—" Jodiah slurred but Pickett scoffed in scandal, so he at least had the good sense to shut his mouth.

Once they were in the hall and sufficiently removed from earshot, Edie was the first to speak. "I changed the contract," she whispered.

Pickett frowned. "Like the trick you used in the inn? You moved the ink around?"

Edie nodded. "I didn't have time to do much, but I was able to ensure Fistic lives. If he dies, all of the Gilt King's holdings and properties revert to Nancy. If she's hurt, he suffers whatever fate befalls her."

"I think I figured out his rune specialty, too," Edie whispered. "He can keep people from going far from him. And he's an expert at tracking."

Suddenly, Pickett was painfully, desperately aware of what he'd put on her neck and how he was planning to keep her close. She forced herself not to let it show as she cleared her throat.

"So if Nancy dies, Patr dies, too?"

"And all their combined holdings are liquidated and turned over to the Ward King of Sedrios."

"Whoever the hell that is." Pickett gave her a queasy smile and nodded. "He behaves himself or he loses it all." It wasn't a guarantee. Patr would no doubt find a way around it if and when he caught the change in the contract. But it bought them a little time.

"What if he can do the same thing?" she asked. "He's a runecaster, too."

Edie shook her head. "He already sent a copy to the Ward King which would keep the one I changed on file."

"So we just need to get them out of here before Patr finds out what you did and forces them to sign an amendment." She'd guess how long it might take for him to do it but, really, she'd never known him at all. It could be an hour. It could be a month. He might never read over it again, or he might read over it right away. But if Pickett was going to be forced to stay behind, she could ensure that he knew about the Nancy change before he sent assassins after them. One advantage to her shit position was that she'd get to see the look on his face when he realized what Edie had done.

Edie paused as they came to the bedroom door. "We shouldn't talk in there," she said. "He might have something to listen in on us."

Did spying count as a form of control? Best to assume so. It made her miss the days before any of this bullshit existed in her life. Pickett planted her hands on her hips. "All right. Let's just trust Simon is clever enough to take care of Jodiah and Nancy. Which means we're responsible for Fistic."

Edie arched a brow. "Well? You used to work here. Is there any place they might have him locked up?"

THIRTY-TWO

The Eloweys didn't have a dungeon. If they did, the lady of the house would have surely thrown Pickett in it after the hair burning incident. What they did have, however, was a series of large cellars. It felt a touch deceitful, leading Edie on like this, letting her think everything was going to be all right, letting her think they'd leave this estate together. She could deal with the guilt of that later, and it'd settle easier if she knew Edie was home and safe again.

After they'd changed back into their usual clothes, flints and all, Pickett led her down the back stairs.

"This is the junk cellar. Mostly, servants used it to deposit whatever they didn't need, which means it's not valuable."

"Making it a decent prison," Edie muttered.

Pickett nodded. "There are probably guards all over the place," she said. "But this is the path the servants use. I doubt Elowey even knows about it and nobody was about to tell her or she might make them clean the steps."

She pulled aside an old tapestry with a display of a woman looking a little too happy to be with a unicorn. Hard to tell if the weaver loved or hated the figure. Behind the cloth was an old wooden door, half-petrified over the years. Pickett jerked her head toward it. "The passage doesn't have any lighting, but it's exactly forty-eight steps down. If you count, you won't trip at the bottom, and there's a lamp I can light down there."

"Wait." Edie grabbed her arm. "Your cape."

"What?"

Edie pointed at her. "The rune cape. You're not wearing it."

Pickett glanced down at herself.

"You can make me a new one," she said. "That one was fucked. At least one of the runes Patr gave you was a lie. You were right about the tracking skill."

Edie sucked in a sharp breath before she spat, "Bastard."

She took the first step down the stairs, then the second. Darkness, dust, and mildew washed over her like a tide.

"What are we going to do when we get back to the bar, though?" Edie asked. "Won't he just come for you?"

Pickett's chest tightened. She forced herself to breathe evenly. "We'll figure that out when we get out of here."

"So how do we get Fistic out of here? If he takes one step in that hall someone's going to see him."

"The same way I used to smuggle sugar out of the larder," Pickett explained. "Apparently, this estate has a grand history of servants undercutting their masters."

"I'm surprised you didn't feel right at home here."

Finally at the bottom, Pickett rested her hand on the latch of the cellar door. It was a simple setup, but if it closed behind them, they wouldn't be able to get out. Not a problem for Edie and Fistic. She was going to smuggle them out the far end of the cellar. But Pickett? Patr would be pissed. Good. Maybe it was time he was reminded just whom he'd married.

She unhooked the latch and stepped through, snapping her fingers at the nearby oil lamp. The spark from her flints fizzled, then caught on the wick, casting the room in a dim, orange glow.

"Don't let the door close all the way," she warned Edie as she took in the cellar. It was hard to see, with the lamplight casting more shadows than it dispelled.

"Fistic," she called taking a step toward the dark.

Heels clicked on the stone.

Pickett jumped back as Corsa emerged from the shadows, her eyes bright in the poor lamp light. She spread her lips, revealing a wide, bright smile. Fuck. When Patr sent her to her station it must have been to guard Fistic. Double fuck with an extra dollop of fuck!

"Clever," Corsa purred. "I wondered if you'd guess where he was. But I'd hoped I was wrong about your judgement."

Corsa stepped forward, her hands spread. There was not yet any shimmer of heat, but the promise of it remained. One wrong move, and they were done for.

Pickett jumped in front of Edie, arms outstretched.

"You can't hurt her without going through me," she snapped. "And Patr wouldn't like for you to go through me."

"I don't need to hurt her," Corsa said smoothly. "I just need you two to turn around, go back up those stairs, and do as you're told."

"So you can imprison us like Nancy?" Edie snapped. "No thanks."

"Don't be so sanctimonious," Corsa scoffed, planting her hands on her hips. "You're here because you took a job for money. Well you have money. Up there, you live in the lap of luxury. More than you could have ever earned on your own."

"What about Gristlark and the other villages he drained dry for that luxury?" Edie demanded. "What if we don't want that?

Corsa grinned, her teeth flashing in the poor light. "Then I just wait. I wait until you're both a hundred yards away from Patr. When your dear protector here can't take another step, I wait until you do. Then I remove you as an obstacle."

A hundred yards. So that was the length of her leash. Pickett's stomach churned and, suddenly, she could taste bile and—

Thunk!

Corsa's eyes went wide, then slid shut as she crumbled to the ground in a heap. Fistic stood behind her, still holding what looked like one of the slats from a heavy oaken barrel.

"That's for my daughter," he said, then spat on her prone form.

Pickett stared at him for a moment, just to make sure. The hair was familiar, even if it had lost its coif. The frame reminded her of Fistic, even if the clothes were a bit stained from dirt and sweat. But the man before her brandishing a slat of wood like a club couldn't possibly be the pampered man with an office full of birds.

Pickett chuckled and began to clap.

"Pickett. Stop," Edie whispered, catching her wrists.

Fistic tucked the slat under his arm. "Show me where I can find my daughter."

"Simon will get her out," Pickett assured him.

"Your buffoon of a brother?"

"Has better access to her than we do," Pickett snapped. "And she's got the wits he doesn't have to make it work. If they get out and she frets about coming back to save you, then she's just getting captured again. Trust your daughter, Fistic."

Fistic glowered down at her, those dark, hungry eyes glittering in the dark. With a growl, he slapped her hand away.

"If she doesn't make it out . . ."

"Then you can get as creative as you like with whatever tantrum you want to throw about it," Pickett said. "For now, I'll show you the way out."

Fistic growled softly but nodded.

Edie, however, turned back to Corsa, and knelt down next to her. "She could follow us."

As Edie touched the unconscious runecrafter's skin, the

runes tattooed on Corsa's hands shuddered, then stilled. "Oh fuck, Pickett, I can't—"

Fistic stood half in shadow, gesturing fiercely at the dark. "Maybe now isn't the time for rune talk."

Pickett threw a glance over her shoulder. It didn't take long to locate a coil of rope and toss it Edie's way. Pickett didn't understand what was wrong with the runes, but she did know how to solve the Corsa following them problem.

"If you've got a handkerchief, maybe shove that in her mouth, too."

"Right." Edie made short work of it, knotting the rope with more speed and skill than Pickett could have hoped. Perhaps, back when she'd been a milkmaid, she'd had other jobs around the farm, too. The whole process only took a minute while Pickett grabbed the oil lamp, holding it aloft to light their path.

"Ready?" Pickett asked.

Edie gave a terse nod and started down the hall.

Just as she remembered, there was the old door, the lock firmly in place. Pickett crouched down, running her hand over the dusty floor until she found her old friend, a rusty nail that had probably been there for years.

"The best thing about old storerooms"—she stuck the nail into the keyhole—"is that they never seem worth the effort to fix them up."

Click!

Pickett grinned and swung open the door, revealing a sharp incline of a tunnel. "This will lead you out into the garden. From there, it's into the treeline. Now, let's get going before that serpent over there wakes up. With any luck it shouldn't be hard for Nancy to find you."

Pickett handed Fistic the lamp, and he plowed through the tunnel. Edie followed right on his heels. Pickett took a step into the tunnel but froze. A sharp sting bit her neck, like the bite of a venomous bug. So this was where the hundred yards ended. Did that mean he'd drag her along on all his business dealings like some sort of pet? It was probably his idea of a happy marriage. She rubbed the back of her neck. Her heart lurched and she had to catch her breath. Fuck. Fuck! She couldn't even have the privacy of a goodbye in the garden. She had to let Edie go right here with an audience.

Edie was halfway up the slope when she paused and glanced over her shoulder.

"Pickett? What's wrong?"

"I . . ." Pickett swallowed around the lump in her throat. "I can't come with you."

Edie's eyes widened and she scrambled back down. "You're the one who said we have to trust Jodiah to do his job."

Pickett shook her head. "It's not that, Edie. I-I really can't come." She tried to spit the truth out. That Patr had stamped his rune on her. That even standing here made her neck sting. But she didn't have to.

Edie frowned. With all the caution of someone approaching a newborn foal, she reached up and pushed Pickett's curls aside. She drew a sharp breath.

"When?"

"When he and I were alone." Pickett's eyes began to burn. She gripped Edie's hand and tried to find the words. But it was like jumping off a cliff while tied to a tree. No matter how much she wanted to throw herself at this, she didn't have it in her.

"Hurry up!" Fistic hissed from the other end of the passage.

Pickett nodded. "You need to go. Get him to safety. Go back to Hoag and Letterboy. Look after the bar."

"I'm not leaving without you."

"We don't have a choice," Pickett insisted, her vision growing blurry. "Besides if I'm here, maybe I can do something. Stop these pigshit operations of his. Keep him from hurting anyone else."

Edie shook her head, some of her blond hair coming loose.

Her hands began to shake in Pickett's. "It's not home without you."

"It'll have to be. I promise I'll find a way to come back. I always do." Pickett smiled wetly and tried to spit the words out. That she loved her. That it was Edie who turned the bar into a home. That it was Edie who brought a spark back into her life. That Pickett would give just about anything to go back to their life together.

All that escaped her was a little gasp.

And then a whimper.

And then there was no need for noise at all as she felt Edie's lips on hers. The cellar burst into light and Pickett's insides turned to sunshine. She grasped Edie's waist as Edie cupped her cheeks.

Edie Edie Edie.

She tasted like wine and apples. She felt like the first day of spring. Pickett barely noticed as their feet moved. As Edie turned her around. As Edie gave her a little push and gods, yes, she could push her anywhere she liked as long as she held on.

And then the contact broke. Her neck felt raw where Edie had touched her in passion. Pickett reached up to feel . . . nothing. The rune was gone.

Pickett blinked and sucked in a sharp breath as she stared at Edie. Edie with the yellow hair and daft ideas. Edie with the big, trusting heart. Edie with tears streaming down her cheeks. Edie who took a step back into the cellar. Pickett's stomach dropped.

"What did you do?" she whispered.

Edie smiled wetly and nodded. "I can't use the torch on your neck like Nancy did on her arm. But I can transfer it." Her voice was so steady, despite her tears.

"Then-then we go put it on Corsa," Pickett insisted. "The bitch has it coming, right?"

Edie touched the back of her neck. "I *can't*," she said, her voice too small for the powerhouse she really was. "Earlier. I tried to put runes on her to bind her, but I couldn't."

"Then we . . ." Pickett fumbled, reaching desperately for an option. Patr? Elowey? Who in this house did they have time to pin it on? "Edie, just give it back to me. He's my husband. I can do this. I can—"

Shouts rang out in the distance followed by the heavy thunder of feet. Pickett thought she could just make out a few words. *Find them. Escape. Fucking dark.*

It sounded like Simon figured out how to use the blackout bottle after all, but of course he had to make a mess of this.

"There's no time," Edie insisted. "They'll come searching down here soon and you need to be gone."

"Corsa will kill you!"

Edie barked out a sharp laugh. "Only if she wants the Gilt King's wrath. He'll keep me alive for your sake. You'll stay alive for mine."

No.

No, this wasn't happening.

She wasn't doing this. Patr had walked away from Pickett. She couldn't walk away from Edie, not after all they'd survived together.

"We'll block the door. We'll find a rat or something."

"Sooner or later they'll come for us. I know the others are already finding a way out. You can't abandon them." Edie touched her cheek. "Please. Trust me."

"Edie."

"The Pick's Pocket needs its witch. I'll save Southfen. Then you save me, all right?" She smiled, her eyes shining in the dark. "I know what it's like to come from a shitty village. Shitty villages don't deserve to be drained by men like him."

"Edie, no!" Pickett shouted, jumping forward, but Edie shoved her bag at Pickett, then slammed the door shut. There was a click of the lock, and then the choked words.

"I love you."

"No!" Pickett threw herself at the door, yanking on the handle, pounding on the wood. Edie was in there. Edie was in there and she had to get her back! She screamed. She begged. She couldn't leave her behind. She couldn't do that. Not to Edie.

Strong arms wrapped around her middle, yanking her back. A light shone from underneath the door. Wood groaned, then swelled outward, pressing into the rock so tight that nothing short of a battering ram could push through it. And Edie was on the other side.

"Time to go!" Fistic shouted.

Pickett screamed and kicked all the way up into the garden.

THIRTY-THREE

Fistic dragged her through the garden and past the treeline, holding her in place until her panic finally gave way to exhaustion. Edie was still in there. Edie, that conniving, rockbrained . . .

The tears came again and Pickett doubled over, her arms wrapped around her middle as she forced herself to breathe through them. Edie was still inside, but by now she was probably out of the cellar, caught in the net that Patr had cast for Pickett. She'd be safe. He wouldn't dare hurt her if she was his hostage. But how long would Edie have to remain his hostage?

Fistic eyed her uneasily.

"That kitchen girl of yours," he said. "I didn't know you had a sorceress on your side."

Pickett shook her head. "She's not," she croaked. "She learned to use runes. Then she took mine off me."

He stared at her for a long moment, then grunted. "She must be very talented. I didn't see her draw one." He gestured vaguely at what could be loosely interpreted as a door, which just made Pickett's gut squirm.

Pickett knew Edie wasn't all powerful and now she was

trapped in the cellar with Corsa. What if Corsa somehow broke through her restraints? She rose and started back toward the cellar, but Fistic caught her by the back of her shirt and dragged her back. Pickett landed on the ground like a sack of potatoes. Edie was in there somewhere. Edie was there and she was here.

"She did this to save you," Fistic insisted. "Do you want to spit on that?"

Did she? Did it fucking matter?

When she didn't answer, Fistic heaved a sigh and ran a hand through his already-mussed hair, pushing some of the dark curls to odd angles as he stared at the house.

"I saw what your friend did to the contract," he murmured. "She's good people. But we need to get Nancy out of there. Once your husband—"

"Don't call him that," Pickett spat.

Fistic paused, looking her up and down. "He's dangerous. If he figures out the change and Nancy doesn't escape." He flexed his hands. "Well? Any clever words? How is my daughter getting out of there?"

Pickett scrubbed a hand over her face. The very notion of having to think of something in that moment ached. She opened her mouth, but she didn't actually know what kind of horse shit she was about to offer. And she didn't need to.

The sound of breaking glass pierced the ear.

Two of the windows flooded with a familiar darkness from Pickett's own jars. She might have laughed if she had it in her. She'd bet right. Simon was smarter than he looked, or else Nancy had taken charge. It was probably Nancy.

Three figures slipped out of the broken window as smoke began to billow behind them, the smell of ash and fire filling the air.

Fistic lurched forward, but Pickett caught his sleeve. If she'd had it in her, she might have laughed. Simon. Fucking Simon. This didn't exactly make up for all the shit he'd pulled in the past, but it had to do something to scrub a couple of spots off his record.

Footsteps rustled through the trees and she rose, just in time to see Nancy throw herself at her father, tears streaming down her round cheeks. She was speaking. Pickett could see her lips moving, but she turned back to stare at the estate. There was a fire in there. Was it anywhere near Patr? Edie? Was Edie going to be all right?

Simon burst through next. More words Pickett didn't care to hear, then he and Fistic shook hands, the bastards. If they'd done that months ago, she and Edie might still be home in the bar.

Then Jodiah stumbled forward, crossbow loose in his grip. By the strain in his expression, she could only guess he'd started to sober up from Lady Elowey's treatment.

"Where's Edie?" he barked.

Edie Edie Edie.

Pickett hugged the bag to her chest. It did nothing to smother the sting.

"She chose to stay behind," she murmured. "Edie decided she wants to be a fucking hero."

"What?" Jodiah's hands began to shake, which wasn't good from someone with a crossbow in his hand and laudanum still in his system. "No. She wouldn't do that."

"Saw it with my own eyes," Fistic said, but a dull ringing began to overtake his words. Pickett turned, staring at the house again. She knew she should probably move. She should think of a way to sneak back in there.

Orange flames peeked through the window. There had to be a roar from it, but she couldn't quite hear it. She could barely smell it. A hand rested on her shoulder. And Edie was still in there. Was she clever enough? Sure, she could stop Pickett and Fistic from getting through the door, but could she keep a fire at a distance?

The hand squeezed her shoulder.

Pickett blinked and glanced over. It was Simon. His lips moved. He gave her a shake, and the ringing softened enough for her to piece together the meaning of all the disparate sounds he was spitting out.

There was a way out.

Nancy stepped forward and spread her skirt. In it rested that precious, ridiculous comb Pickett never should have stolen, along with other small treasures someone like Elowey would never have thought to protect: brass handles and knobs and a small carved-amber cameo. Maybe she liked Simon because she knew she was smarter than him. Maybe they'd planned it together. Either way, it was a good idea.

Jodiah rested a hand on her shoulder. "How long do we need to wait for Edie?"

How long? Too fucking long.

"She can't leave," Pickett whispered. She turned her back to the estate. The orange glow from within had softened as the smoke belched from the building grew lighter and thinner, more steam than smoke. How many people had been hurt before they got the fire under control? How long until they determined what could be salvaged? Had they already gone down to the basement to find Edie? She took a step forward but met Jodiah's arm. Despite the lingering laudanum, he was strong. In half an hour, he could probably take her down. Even now, he could stop her from going back in. The fucker.

"Edie wouldn't want you to get caught again," he snapped. "If you get caught or killed, you can't find a way out of this. You need to regroup somewhere safe and make a new plan. Staying here won't help her."

It wouldn't, would it? What was it Edie had said? Pickett scrubbed a hand over her face and nodded.

"Right," she muttered. "Edie will save Southfen. I'll find a way to save her."

Jodiah took a deep breath and puffed out his chest. "She won't save Southfen alone," he said. "I swear on Al-Dagos and all the gods of the Untamed. She won't come to harm. You just do your part and find a way through this maze."

"You're crazy," Simon cried, but Nancy caught his arm.

She locked eyes with Jodiah and, whatever passed between them had to be a thing for religious folks because they both nodded in tandem.

"May the great dragon grant you wisdom," she said.

"May she guide us unto the path," he replied.

Jodiah turned and, with all the grace of an oak-branched scarecrow, began to limp back toward the Elowey estate. The fool. The damn fucking fool. Pickett sucked in a lungful of air and held it until it turned to fire in her chest. Edie wanted her to go, so she'd go. Edie wanted her to live, so she'd live. If that meant building up the will to drive an arrow through Patr's eye, then she'd do that.

Fistic squeezed her shoulder. When Pickett began to shuffle forward, he did, too.

She remembered walking, first across a path then down a hill. Then cobblestones. The stink of a city, then of fish, then of the sour ocean. Simon and Nancy darted forward to a small skiff whose owner had just finished unloading the day's catch. Fistic gripped her shoulder, but he didn't need to. He overestimated how much energy she had to get involved.

Edie was trapped in that cellar, and Pickett was with family. Stonebrained family, sure. But they were safe and she was free and Edie was not.

Pickett settled down among the nets and crates on the deck, still hugging the bag to her chest. The ship began to sail up one of the inlets that flowed from the swamplands. They were taking her back to the bar, but Edie wasn't with her.

"Where to?" the skiff-owner grunted.

"The Rottering swamp," Pickett muttered. "There's a bar in the middle of it."

"Sonora, that'll be the first place he comes looking for you," Simon objected.

Pickett took a deep breath. "Edie went home to speak to a friend. Her words." Pickett swallowed and touched her neck, now free of Patr's mark. "Whoever he was, I want to talk to him. Besides, I know a man who knows a swamp beast. I'll be fine."

Simon and Nancy shared a look, but neither tried to argue. As the owner unfurled his sail, the pair crept up to the bow, presumably to steal a few precious moments for themselves. And there was Fistic, hovering around her like a dog eyeing a rabbit.

At long last, he settled onto the crate next to her, his hands on his knees.

"We'll all smell like fish by the time we get to your bar," he mused. "Interesting. The Pick's Pocket has been an investment of interest for me for some time. I'll be glad to finally see it with my own eyes."

Pickett grunted.

He tilted his head toward her. "For what it's worth, it is a difficult thing. Business. Loyalty. Love. They don't tend to mix well. Eventually, you choose what you will or won't drop."

Pickett let her head drop against the wooden side of the ship, staring up at the stars.

"You chose business over love. You hired a runecrafter to lock your daughter away from love."

"And I don't think I'll regret it in the long run. Nor will your friend."

Pickett swallowed thickly. "She didn't even give me a choice."

He shrugged. "Of the two of you, she's in more of a position to keep that man at bay. And I think she knows it. Or maybe she just didn't want you to be a prisoner. Choose which one you want to believe until you see her again." He leaned toward her. "In the meantime, my empire has fallen. Your bar's headed for rough times, and I don't like to think what a man like him will do to the city. Can we count on you to help restore the natural order?"

The natural order led to her father most likely being killed because of money. That same order had put her in so much debt that she had to be indentured to finish paying it off. The system left her broke and desperate enough to buy a fishing shack off a stranger. That order took a sweet sailor and dragged all his dark innards out so he could bleed towns dry and hold women hostage. The order wasn't natural at all. It was fucked.

Pickett didn't answer. Fistic deflated a little, but had the good sense not to push as they headed into the swamps.

THIRTY-FOUR

P ull down the sail," the captain barked. "We're headed into boardwalk territory. Gotta go slow."

The stink of the Rottering swamp washed over the vessel well before the boardwalks came into view. Pickett sat up a little straighter. As the captain instructed Jodiah and Simon to switch to oars, the vessel began to weave around the network of boardwalks. Here and there, she could already see where patches of the walkways had been replaced with fresh wood, and where others were rotting away. And there, in the distance was home.

When she'd first seen it, she'd been an underfed thing too eager to have a roof over her head. One that would actually belong to her. One she couldn't lose to someone else's neglect. Every last coin she'd scrounged up working here and there as she traveled back down from Coldspine went into that fisherman's hands. And he didn't so much as breathe a word of warning to her.

That first night after the fisherman sold her the place, she slept on the floor and didn't feel at home at all. Even after she took the loan from Fistic and set up a bar and tables and got in rum and beer, it was just a place.

Then a frightened girl with yellow hair burst through the door.

The boat came to a stop just next to the boardwalk. Pickett shuffled forward and heaved herself up. Simon hesitated then rose.

"Do-do you want me to stick around?" he offered.

"This is the last place any of you needs to be."

"The same goes for you," Nancy pointed out from her seat next to her father. "You should come with us."

"And abandon my bar?" Pickett scoffed. "It's fine. I have Hoag and Letterboy. Besides, if he's focused on me he's less likely to focus on any of you. At least we know he doesn't want to kill me."

Simon nodded and lurched forward, grabbing her in a quick hug before she could pull back. He then grabbed his oar and helped Nancy, Fistic, and the boat's owner to head on to wherever it was they were going. Pickett realized then she never had asked. Well, she'd find out or she wouldn't.

Nancy and Simon tried to wave at her, and Pickett raised her hand in a halfhearted salute before she trudged through the doors and into the bar. Someone was at the stage, his head flung back as he balanced the tip of a dagger on his teeth while a fiddler sawed on his instrument and the crowd clapped in time. The hunters at the table nearest to the door glanced up, and one visibly sighed in relief.

"Thank the winds around us. Can you make us a proper drink, dear? Your friend's not exactly as skilled as you."

"Later," Pickett mumbled as she dragged herself to the bar. Hoag stood behind it, placidly rubbing the inside of a cracked glass with a rag. He brightened as she approached.

"My lady sorceress. The waters told me your journey would soon end."

"Yeah. For now." Pickett squeezed Edie's bag. It didn't do anything, really, but at this point, it made her feel better. "Good to see the bar's still operating."

"Loyal bunch, these folks," he said solemnly. "Kind souls."

"You do know they're bounty hunters, don't you?"

Hoag furrowed his brows. Then Pickett could only assume he wiped the fresh information from his mind because he settled back into a pleasant expression and nodded.

"Kind souls."

"Sure." Pickett heaved a heavy sigh. "Edie was just back to speak to a friend. Where can I find him?"

"Edie?" Letterboy popped up from behind the bar, his eyes wide. "Is Edie back?"

Pickett swallowed thickly. "She'll be along. Hoag?"

He scratched the side of his nose. "No friend that I can recall. She came. She told me I had to add your sour juice to the rum. She packed that bag and she left." He cocked his head to the side. "Why do you have her bag? It's hers."

Hoag wasn't getting it, but Letterboy was. His expression faltered and he looked Pickett up and down. He was so young to get things so clearly.

"When will she be along?"

Pickett held out a hand. "Gimme a bottle of rum."

He handed it over solemnly. Pickett took it and stalked over to the corner, where Edie had set up her museum of oddities. The peg-legged woman bent over a plate, in deep communication with a scarred man.

"Fuck off," she said. "I'm gonna sit here."

"That's not very hospitable of you," the woman snapped. "Swamp witch or not."

"Tell Hoag at the bar you can each have a beer on the house." Pickett made a shooing motion with her hand. The two hunters glanced at each other then moved. Pickett plopped down in the booth and uncorked the bottle.

"You shouldn't do that."

Pickett froze. The fiddle stopped. The crowd cheered. Three sheets to the wind and ready to sing, the next hunter tottered onto the stage. She shook her head. That was strange, but she'd been through a lot. She was going to drink herself into a stupor and pass out. When she was over the hangover, maybe she'd be refreshed enough to handle what was in front of her.

The singer started slurring out a few lyrics. Pickett lifted the bottle to her lips.

"I'm serious. You need to be sober for what comes next."

Pickett started, nearly dropping the bottle onto the ground. Letterboy stared at her from the bar, not even trying to hide his concern. Maybe he ought to be concerned because she was pretty fucking sure she could hear a voice coming from right behind her.

Pickett glanced over her shoulder. Sure enough, there was nothing but the dried up swamp grass and that ugly turtle skull with the chipped plaster horns.

And as she stared at it, the voice echoed inside of her head again.

"Took you long enough to notice me. Will you get this plaster off me? Edie's a doll but I don't do dress-up."

Pickett shrieked and jumped back, knocking her bottle to the floor.

"Pickett!" Letterboy made to run in her direction, but Hoag rested a hand on his shoulder.

"Leave her be, boy," he said solemnly. "That's witch business."

Pickett glanced around wildly. The people at the table nearest to her rose, inching toward the nearest empty table on the other side of the bar. She turned back to the skull, heart in her throat.

"So you're who Edie came back for?" she murmured, looking

the thing up and down, left and right. "Why the fuck would she think you could help her?"

"Because my name is Skilp and I'm her friend."

"And you can talk," she whispered.

Its boney face didn't move, but its voice pitched a little.

"Obviously. But only to Edie. Well, now and you, I suppose. Or maybe only you."

"Kelp?"

"Skilp."

"Yes. Of course. My mistake." She reached for the rum bottle, half of which had drained out onto her floor. Perfect way to end the night. "And is there a reason you don't want me to empty this tonight, Skilp?"

"Because Edie trusted me to you. And you'll need your wits if we're going to get her back."

Acknowledgments

As always, a huge thank you to my agent Ann and editor Kelly for bringing me into this wonderful universe and keeping me from going off the deep end, and to Kevin for creating Sedrios in the first place!

About the Author

C.M. McGuire may or may not be a cryptid living in central Texas, spoken of only in hushed whispers in small circles. It is said she holds degrees in history and creative writing and, when away from her word processor, teaches. This can only be corroborated by her elderly dog and 2 cats, but thus far they are tight-lipped.

JOIN THE CURSED DRAGON SHIP NEWSLETTER

Love what you just read? Want more just like it? Sign up for our newsletter so you don't miss out on the adventure. You'll get:

- A free book for signing up
- Advanced notice of new releases
- First word of books on sale
- Opportunities for free books
- Most up-to-date information on author appearances.

We're busy and know you are too. We won't send more than one newsletter a month.

Register below.

CHECK OUT THE ANTHOLOGY FEATURING CHARACTERS FROM EACH MA SERIES

A card cursed with self-awareness seeks a hero to retrieve his creator from the afterlife. Nothing could possibly go wrong.

CHECK OUT THE SERIES THAT STARTED IT ALL

Stealing the cash box of your mercenary unit as you run away probably isn't wise, but it sure is funny.